Hollywood

&

Hardwood

Also by Tricia Bauer

Boondocking

Working Women and Other Stories

HOLLYWOOD

&

HARDWOOD

TRICIA BAUER

Bridge Works Publishing Company
Bridgehampton, New York

Published in the United States by Bridge Works Publishing Company, Bridgehampton, New York.
Distributed in the United States by National Book Network, Lanham, Maryland.

First Edition

"Petitions" was first published in *The Beloit Fiction Journal* and "New House" in the New Rivers Press anthology *The Next Parish Over*, both in somewhat different form.

Library of Congress Cataloging-in-Publication Data

Bauer, Tricia.
    Hollywood & hardwood: a novel / Tricia Bauer. — 1st ed.
       p.   cm.
    ISBN 1-882593-26-X (alk. paper)
    I. Title.   II. Title: Hollywood and hardwood.
  PS3552.A83647H65   1999
  813'.54 — dc21   98-43998
                                            CIP

2   4   6   8   10   9   7   5   3   1

Book and jacket design by Eva Auchincloss

Printed in the United States of America

For Bozzone

"I've married over two hundred couples in my day.
Do I believe in it?
I don't know.
. . . Once in a thousand times it's interesting."

— Thornton Wilder's *Our Town*

CONTENTS

I

Between Them

1

Vermont

OVERNIGHT, JULY IN VERMONT cools to the moldy breath of a basement beneath moaning wide-board floors. Once I saw a man taste water samples from each of the Great Lakes and then identify the five correctly. Just by smell, I could distinguish Vermont from all the New England states.

WHEN I FIRST SPOTTED YOU in White Birch Lodge, you were opening an old refrigerator made sometime deep in the '50s and sliding in a couple of six-packs. The beers were icy and sleek, exotic against the growing heat of late morning. You were the playwright; I was the actress, and this was summer stock.

THE ACTORS HAD BEEN uttering your phrases for two days across the stark stage, against the clatter of insects and birdsong. I wanted you to notice that I took great care with your words, with the particular way they left my lips.

THE FIRST PLACE we touched was the fingertips, the extremities that moved so many things. I was holding the script while your index finger slid along the monologue, stopped at the word "more". All the lines crossing and crisscrossing and zigzagging over my skin shifted to one direction, focused at a single point.

AT NIGHT WE SAT on a log of white oak that, if it had been a container, could just about have held us. Our legs dangled off the side, well above the ground as if we were both kids again. The studio, big as a barn, loomed behind, but the whine of saw and click and chip of tools had stopped. The smell of fresh-cut wood hung strong as peeled fruit.

We talked about stage directions. You invented new ones just for then; you talked me closer to you. Next came the softness — lips and breasts and hands — and then beneath me — sawdust. Sawdust in my hair and eyes, your mustache. . . . Sawdust under my fingernails. We ground everything between us to its smallest part.

WHEN I FIRST WOKE was the only time I could see myself with some objectivity. What was happening felt as if it had all been planned. The men, the parts I'd played, jobs and classes I'd taken, comprised marks in a long dotted line to Vermont.

YOU MADE ME HUNGRY. I became an animal for the first time. But I could not put even a piece of lettuce to my lips without thinking of your lips on my lips. I couldn't chew without stimulating myself into a frenzy.

EVEN AS I WAS kissing you, I knew I didn't want you to be the way my life would change. I needed an audience to catch up with my ambition, propel me out onto the huge arena where the applause never quits. And yet the intense connection between us pressed me to give everything to it.

I PROWLED ACROSS the stage hungry. I was hungry when I sat perfectly still in my little room, my shirts and pants and underthings strewn across the floor in a path to the bed.

THE FIRST TIME I was kissed, I was Emily. As soon as I said, I always expect a man to be perfect and I think he should be," I started to anticipate the kiss even though there was nearly another scene-and-a-half to go. I waited for the touch of George's mouth to automatically make my eyes close.

Every time that George leaned into me and made his mark, I felt a trickle through my body all the way to my feet. I couldn't become part of a man who'd entice me to forget college and my plans to become an actress, just to stay home to work his farm.

The first night *Our Town* had an audience, the director told me I looked as though I'd been kissing for years.

MAKING LOVE, I WAS afraid I'd fall so far into myself I'd disappear. But you said it was like diving into deep water: I'd resurface and come back wanting to do it again and again.

IN THE GRAVEYARD I found the first sign.

Although we couldn't locate your last name — Italians aren't much of a presence in northern Vermont — we discovered a Lou and Renata, husband and wife.

The ragweed stood hip-high around headstones. Nothing moved, not branches overhead, not the river or the bits of wildflowers flung on its surface. Looking at lives that had passed, I thought only of that moment. No edges to break the softness. No boundaries to mean we had gone too far.

Why do lovers think constantly of their death? Was it because just before I arrived in Vermont I'd researched traffic accidents as back story for an audition and I'd come to look at everyone as a potential statistic? Or did I somehow foresee that eventually our every motion, every conversation, would become a symbol for shedding hallowed solitude? For evolving. For choosing dialogue over monologue?

A crow squawked my name. Then the others tossed it among themselves until we left that place.

I RECITED MY FAVORITE monologues to you. You held my hand and listened until I spoke one of your own. And then your hands moved to my neck, worked their way down my body. "This," you said, "is the only language."

IN BED YOU ASKED me if I believed in marriage. I hadn't, but I did.

My mother said WAIT. My friends said WAIT. The minister I had known since I was fifteen said, "I think you should think about this some more. A week you've known him. It's only been a week." The snob that I worked for at Chesapeake Caterers said, "Well, the Italians *did* discover America."

I was suspicious of the minister, who said his first available Saturday was in October, but we booked him anyway.

Our only plan was to marry outside, beyond the cloak of religious garments and crosses and pedestals, but on the day of the wedding it poured. My father held a huge multi-colored golf umbrella over me as we made our way to the chapel and I was giggling by the time I spotted you. You were drinking scotch (you hate scotch) and grinning.

The entire front wall of the chapel became a giant window to the fall forest. I imagined that this was Vermont and not the suburbs of Baltimore. Silently I identified the changing trees — beech, oak, sycamore, oak, maple, oak — an incantation to calm myself. Everything I heard and repeated was part of a play bigger than I could have imagined.

In the middle of the "I do"s, a dog trotted through the outdoor scene. Sniffed. All of us followed the narrative as if it were part of our movie. The animal squatted for the longest time, then kicked the leaves into a flurry of color. Immediately after the service, everyone was talking about the dog. No one was sure if this was a good omen, happening the moment we promised ourselves each to the other.

They made bets. My old roommate. My brother. My mother. Two years. Two months. Six weeks.

AFTER A BLUR of dancing and champagne and gifts, we drove as far as we could, heading north. In mountains, in Pennsylvania, we stopped.

"Any rooms?"

"Yeah, sure."

The small town of stuttering cars and closed store-fronts and heat-eaten lawns dissolved when we opened the door to our room, steeped in light. A delicate wall pattern of peach- and gold-colored flowers and stems resembled the wrapping paper of our wedding gifts, and in the center of the room — a huge white circle of bed. *You are here.* Everything smelled brand new. The pale gauzy curtains swelled into the room and retreated on the unseasonably warm day. Something immense breathing just beyond us.

"Did anybody know we'd stop here?"

"*We* didn't know." We hadn't known how far we could drive before we'd need to touch each other.

I WOKE BESIDE YOU before the room turned morning gray; it was still black and bitten by stars. A husband is more than a place to store your emotions until you can produce a child. Even then, I knew this.

HONEYMOON WAS ONLY the beginning.

The next summer we returned — lots of people lost bets — to Vermont for *Peer Gynt,* and the huge oak log had been transformed. No longer a piece of tree christened with sawdust, it was a sculpture. An abstraction, maybe of a woman's body. Though nothing like the set where we were first alone, both of us recognized it instantly.

THE FIRST DREAM WE had together wasn't a scene from some play we'd talked about earlier but a boat in very clear water. Below us, red fish swam by.

Before long I woke in the middle of a conversation. It was my own voice that startled me, and yours, in sleep, answering back.

Sometimes a thought came defiantly clear to me: it doesn't matter which of us speaks, which of us dreams, which of us becomes famous.

What was between us moved with such confidence it took on a glow, then a golden color when we stood next to each other. It was a thing apart from either of us and yet an integral part, like the way I understood the Holy Ghost.

FIVE YEARS AGO, we visited the first place we lived together in Greene, Vermont. We dreamed about this place so often I worried we'd worn the shabby rug off its scarred and painted hardwood floor, shattered the flimsy French doors that quaked with every rumor of winter, punched my feet through the three soggy steps to the front door. I thought that maybe the old house had been torn down and we could save just what we wanted of it.

On the third pass-by, you finally said, "I can't believe it." And there, the building the color of a January sky, heavy with snow but not snowing, was the house that had held our apartment. Its shutters were slate blue, boxes for pansies and nasturtiums punctuated the windows. A new balcony. A wrap-around porch with columns. Out back, a Mercedes protruded from the garage.

"What does this mean?" I screamed at nothing in particular.

"This," you said, "is proof."

THE MOST INTERESTING THING about this story is that nobody wants to believe it. Not even me at first. At first, I thought one of us would die or both of us would die together in a weird-world story, like driving to see each other the night before the wedding or the night after the honeymoon. Captured forever in the tight grip of romance.

Everybody thinks of chucking it all and moving to where we are, but. . . . The big but.

After these many years, a two-day courtship should have tightened to a trickle of romance, squeezed thin by the demands of children and work and just the way the world moves. Consuming love is kept stored in movies.

There are new ways to describe what goes on and on without quitting — deluded, co-dependent, but they're just words.

So, I don't say much. As marriages fall apart around me like planned obsolescence, and kids devour their parents' passion, and a TV movie is made of every twist on tragedy, I keep quiet. All the lines that used to jerk into different directions, then straightened out to a purpose when I met you, now swirl over me in one watery direction. I am now so far out of myself I can see my little body, my mouth small and still as a doll's. I could play the part of the tiny dark spot in an eye, the period in a sentence. But then I see you and lose all perspective. At once I'm clumsy and soft and ecstatic inside my huge self.

2

Hardwood

The first thirteen months of our marriage we made love every day, sometimes two and three times a day. In between sex, Lou wrote plays and I wrote obituaries for the newspaper in Burlington, Vermont, and read the complete works of Shakespeare, memorizing monologues. We read and wrote until we were dizzy, and then sex — where we moved with the grace and energy of competitive swimmers — would empty us completely.

The winter we made the decision to go over the line of family expectations, the two-room cottage we'd recently begun renting seemed charged with the reverberations of our bodies and artistic ambitions, along with the furnace running continuously against the unrelenting New England cold. Neither of us wanted to say, I know enough of you. So we kept up — peeling off each other's clothes, kissing our way to bigger yearnings, falling exhausted across the double bed that filled the entire second room.

And then we ran out of fuel oil.

"Call them up, Renata," Lou said, reciting the number affixed to the huge rust-colored tank.

I phoned them and every other listing under OILS-FUEL in the yellow pages. Everyone wanted cash payment on delivery of their product. Between us, Lou and I generally worked twenty-seven hours a week, which just about got us by.

Lou went off. "What ever happened to credit in this damn country?"

"My mother and her neighbors are hoarding it," I said. Those women still put outfits on layaway, and all year paid for Christmas gifts with fistfuls of plastic. In their prioritizing of non-tangible assets, credit ranked just below citizenship and slightly above education.

"We'll have to think of something," Lou said.

SOMEHOW YOU NEVER IMAGINE that the temperature inside a house, even a rented cottage, can quite match the snowy expanse immediately beyond it. The sidewalk layered with cracked ice, the brittle clusters of branches burdened with months' accumulation of flurries, the slick glassy hollow beneath a parked car. Certainly not within a tiny house armed with a stove and a television and lamps and the soft lumps of a couch, which had been in the family for generations, and yards of books shielding ivory-colored walls.

But the cottage became so cold that finally we moved the table from the front of the old fireplace and worked the cap off the chimney. Then Lou checked through all our coat pockets for money to buy starter logs, while I contemplated arrangements of furniture that wouldn't induce somebody's hair to catch fire when we were watching TV. Lou came back with "Cozy Coal".

"Let's give it a try," he said with enthusiasm.

That night I dreamed of trains sliding into the long tunnel of night. I got off and on different ones, each direction as dark as the next. Though I listened for announcements of town names I recognized, no final destination sounded familiar enough for me to stay on board. By morning, the cottage smelled as if the locomotives of my dreams had stalled three feet from our bed. But it was warm. At least until we opened all five windows of the place to set the thick oily air loose on the neighborhood.

"We've got to talk," I said a couple of hours later when we were scouting up small pieces of rotting wood in the acres behind the cottage. But instead of debating how our lives had to change, Lou tackled me from behind and we dropped onto the frozen ground. Even the decayed wood covering the forest floor was hard with winter.

"Talk, talk, talk," Lou whispered, taking my face in his hands. The lacy canopy of evergreens above him brightened and then, as I concentrated on his lips, went out of focus.

LOU'S INITIAL, somewhat startled, "You're not getting out of bed today?" became a routine question, and then not a question at all. I brought Shakespeare into bed with me, eventually slipping out only for my daily stint at the newspaper and for meals, though sometimes I sipped milk and ate sandwiches in bed, too. And, of course, I waited for Lou to join me and send me wallowing in the heat of our own bodies.

Lou set a quart of beer on the windowsill.

"I don't know. I just have no taste for it," I said.

"This is new," he said. He stared at me.

LOU CONTINUED TO GATHER scrap wood from the forest beyond the cottage. He found a bow saw behind the furnace and used it to cut the larger pieces. He sought out hardwoods, which burn hot and long.

"Look at these babies," he said, holding out a pile of oak logs with pride. When he added a piece of locust to the fire, it smelled as though we were burning a mixture of old clothes and garbage.

"I think this is all the hardwood. We'll have to go for pine next," he said.

"Pine's got to smell better," I commented.

"Like turpentine," he said.

"I feel nauseous," I said.

Under the weight of flannel sheets and quilts and covers, with the smoke of the fireplace catching at the back of my throat, I imagined the values Lou and I had been born to lifting off us. Settle down; get an "honest" job; save money for "when you might really need it"; raise a family so you have some proof of your love. I felt us turning away from our past as surely as if a door were closing behind us and a more secret one lay ahead.

To become more resolute about forging our way toward the unexpected curve and bend, we agreed to abstain from the one pleasure that sustained us — sex.

We decided that the passion binding us in our quest to leave the place where we were born shouldn't distract us from our resolution. For one week we would hold ourselves from touching each other. We woke in tight, breathless embraces we were quick to shake off. I looked away from any hint of softness in Lou's eyes. Certain deprivations, we thought, would encourage clearness of thought. And we wanted to make a ceremony of this decisive time in our lives.

"What do you say, Ren?"

"We have three more days."

"Four days is long enough." He was running his middle finger along the inside of my forearm.

"What's our decision then?" I asked.

"You decide," he said, kissing me on the side of the neck.

"That's not fair," I said though I ached to pull him to me. To feel my face in his hands, then my neck and breasts and waist and hips and calves, then finally my feet, high overhead, in his hands.

That sexless week, I became so focused on my ambition to act that my bodily drives metastasized. I envisioned myself as hundreds of different women, all caught within a choice — Desdemona, Juliet, Cordelia. . . . I thought of those women as I took my lunch at work in the small sitting area adjoining the ladies' room of the newspaper. The door between the two rooms had swollen to outmatch the frame. I'd eat and read and contemplate as countless women relieved themselves, flushed, washed their hands and left. Every once in a while someone would invade my sanctuary to use the mirror. The reporter who wrote wedding announcements for Sunday's paper always commented on the number of obituaries I'd done as if we were in some kind of competition.

I considered myself to be marking time, waiting for something or someone to propel me in one direction or another. And it felt fitting for me to be physically positioned at such an elemental level. The decision had departed the intellect and become one more function of the body. I thought briefly of my own body — changing.

I waited for the quiet that settled almost like smoke after the women finished. Sunlight sliced through the murky windows and warmed the back of my neck. My coworkers had no idea that I was debating the reasons people step aside from a life of complementary colors and practical cars onto a path where dreams would not be sublimated by expensive attractive possessions. Lou and I were seduced by the unknown, where love and ambition might destroy each other. And us.

I knew we had to make a decision before there was no decision for us to make.

Lou fit a piece of our wood from the last pile into the fireplace. "What we should have is a wood stove," he said.

"If we had the money for a stove, we could buy the damn oil," I reminded him. Both of us were testy after a week of no sex.

He stood up quickly and turned to me, almost accused me, "Do you want me to take a regular full-time job, Renata? Because if you want me to take a regular job, I'll do it." He sighed. "I'll do anything."

I fell against the soft, smoky-smelling couch. He made the words "regular job" sound like a resounding defeat, a step into the dank hole of his past. "Regular job" for Lou seemed like too much of a sacrifice and yet, what about my "regular" — if part-time — job? Was I to join that army of women who waited tables or worked at clerical jobs to put husbands through medical school or to support them until they got that first break?

In our grand plan, my time had almost arrived to audition in New York. Lou had nearly finished his play about a man who methodically cut down all the trees on his property. But my own body, not my husband, betrayed me.

At first, you don't think of a decision physically pushing you over a line. You do what you do every day until you have a routine that makes you feel as if you're standing still. But actually, you've set something in motion that circles you, almost protectively, like a moon. And gradually, you're moving closer and closer to the edge, stretching off into foreign directions. When you finally recognize yourself pressed there against the line, so sharp it can catch ordinary light and turn it into a weapon, you begin to sweat. Something irrevocable is about to happen.

I started to eat more — breads and pasta and rice dishes. I dressed myself in layers of clothing that not only warmed me as we eked out our pile of available wood but buffered me temporarily from all that lay ahead.

I sketched the house where I hoped one day we'd live — a big place and warm, with a furnace breathing deeply through our rooms. I squared off the interior into blueprint-like spaces, leaving extravagant rectangles for our individual studios. A dotted line opened onto a stage.

We kept our clothes under the bed in suitcases, which we slid in and out like cumbersome drawers. This makeshift dresser reminded us of our temporary situation, that we wouldn't be living in Vermont for long. As soon as Lou rewrote his play, we would move to Manhattan. There he'd shop *Woods We Know* and I would audition for every production that called for women in their twenties.

But then Lou started to rethink our agenda, to mention alternatives, "other" ways.

"Come on, Bonnie," he said.

"Who's Bonnie?" I asked.

"Bonnie and Clyde," he said.

LOU BORROWED MONEY from his brother in Florida.

Lou held my hand as we walked into the austere medical building, its angles sharp, its color that of dried blood. Every one of its bricks was distinctive. The cold air pulled tightly around us; there was no turning away from the glass door. I couldn't hear a passing car or our feet against the loose gravel in the parking area but sensed only my heartbeat, fast and steady.

We entered the white room and there Lou left me alone for forty-six minutes.

We loved each other, craved and covered each other's bodies with extraordinary touch, but what we wanted to produce was not of our bodies. This is what I thought as I lay on my back on the gurney and stared at the decal of a butterfly on the ceiling. The plastic spotted wings and thick antennae weren't subtle enough to be real. And they didn't seem out of place.

Then I heard instruments clatter. They caught the light like a collection of polished heirlooms. The nurse circled me. Though her hands were cool, I began to sweat. I felt the prick of a needle and I tried to match my breathing to the rhythmic hiss of some machine at the source of things.

Afterward, Lou reappeared and led me to the car. In the parking lot I threw up a few spermlike dribbles. Emptied myself completely before we started our lives anew.

We didn't talk but Lou kept his hand on my knee like an anxious, doting adolescent and moved it only to shift into higher gears. He wound each gear out as long as he could before changing position to engage the clutch.

When I pointed at a couple of pieces of firewood that must have fallen from a delivery truck overloaded with cords, Lou pulled off the road. From the car I watched him retrieving them. He handed the wood to me through my open window. Holding the pieces on my lap, I pulled off my gloves and carefully touched the fresh cuts in the wood. Hundreds of tiny interior lines all turned and straightened out together in a lovely purposeful pattern. Within minutes, the sweet odor of cherry wood filled our car.

3
Petitions

For years we went through the rituals. To get a good review, I'd hold a lucky token of the play he'd written (a bouquet of red and pink roses, a hammer and nails, a tiny plastic hamburger) or wear socks I'd worn on past fortunate days, or mumble promises of denial (no pre-dinner drinks on weeknights, no sleeping past 6 A.M.) into the black void of the stage just before the lights came up.

Sometimes the techniques worked and sometimes they didn't but I always went along with Lou's suggestions. We needed every bit of luck. I had just finished playing Tuba, a manic-depressive Danish musician, in a play no reviewer had wandered far enough downtown to see. Lou was in the middle of previews for his own play that had taken years to write and weeks to name. Soaking in the bathtub together, Lou and I had gone through titles as if naming a baby.

The day before *Ever More* was to be reviewed by *The New York Times,* Lou said, "We've got to go all out this time, Renata." He spoke with such resolve that I knew the next few days would be intense, fueled with more anxiety than I'd felt playing Tuba. Lou was thirty-five and ready for a change, for this play to be the one to propel us out of years of methodic struggle. He wanted me to quit my temp job, and to leave Tylor Correctional, the maximum-security prison where for ten hours a week he taught criminals how to assemble words into sentences of salvation. More than bad reviews, we were tired of being overlooked, tired of appraisals that ignored hard work and sacrifice.

Lou had been superstitious since the day I met him nine years earlier but now he wanted to actively entice the spiritual. "I know you're going to think this is weird," he said, "but I'd like to plant a bottle of booze in the yard."

"That's fine but we have no yard." Sometimes he needed to be reminded of the most obvious things, like our two-room, sixth floor walk-up.

"The courtyard," he said, grinning.

"The courtyard? Lester will be on it like a dog scouting a steak bone." That elderly, first-floor resident told stories about his once-generous efforts to improve inter-cultural understanding. He said that he'd handed out three hundred Kennedy silver dollars when he'd been vacationing in Dublin, and another time had distributed a knapsack full of NASA Apollo patches from atop Mount Fuji. But these days Lester was on the receiving end of such gestures. People frequently set bags of clothing or food up against the entrance to his apartment, and the donations fell into his apartment like a sigh of relief when he opened the door.

"Well, we have to think of something. I've got a bottle of vodka just waiting to do its work."

"Did you get good stuff?"

Lou ignored the question and went on to explain how, during a recent volcanic eruption in Hawaii, a man had buried a bottle of alcohol as a petition to the gods. Shortly after making his offering, the flow of hot lava stopped sixteen feet from his house. Experts weren't able to explain the phenomenon in any scientific way.

When I didn't respond to the story immediately, Lou

said, "But the poor guy lost his house anyway." The man's neighbors, whose houses had all been destroyed by the eruption, couldn't understand why one man was spared. "They got all worked up one night and burned his house down."

"That's very interesting," I said, "but the guys we're talking about aren't gods. They're critics." It was easy to say since I'd escaped a public assessment of Tuba.

"I'm talking about gods, Ren," Lou said. "We have to get to the gods first."

After a few beers we decided to bury the bottle an hour north of New York City, at Lou's sister's house in Putnam County.

DURING EACH OF LOU'S plays, I sat by myself while he paced the back of the theater. Sometimes, seated at the end of a row, I'd feel his arm suddenly emerge from the darkness. Frequently it was as moist and shaky as something newborn. He'd drum his fingers along my skin until I was sure I'd find bruises when the lights came up. After those brief moments of physical contact, he'd retreat to the bowels of the theater.

Just before the Wednesday performance of Lou's show, the stage manager whispered to me, "It's HIM." To my left sat *The New York Times'* drama critic. The man pulled a briefcase onto his knees and with two clicks it surrendered its inner secrets. He withdrew a pen as if he were about to sign a multi-figure contract, pulled his pants legs up with two quick plucks, then snapped his pen into position the moment the lights went down. The reviewer had the assurance of someone who'd set a trap and had only to wait for his prey to meander into it.

I had every intention of laughing enthusiastically and clapping hard, but the professionalism of the man beside me was intimidating. He made no gestures, few notes, not even a growl of assent or disgust. Sweat trickling down the inside of my arms, I imagined I was melting.

Without lingering to see if he applauded after the first act, I slipped away at intermission. Backstage, cigarettes puffed frantically smoked like an explosion. The actors crossed their fingers and legs, giggled nervously or stared into space. Lucinda, the female lead, was tall and blonde and usually appeared completely poised. Tonight, she picked absently at her nails and hair, mumbled her lines, sporadically chanting, "Oh my God, oh my God," with religious fervor.

"Damn," Lou said to me. "Who in the hell told them the *Times* was here tonight?" Lou didn't like actors forewarned of a critic's presence, which he said could reduce the most experienced actor to a groveling lackey, bereft of character and forgetful of blocking and other actors.

"Calm down," I advised him, though I knew my advice was as useless as my seat next to the reviewer.

During the second act, I paid particular attention to the man in the three-piece suit beside me. I never looked him directly in the face; I memorized the mellow, pervasive scent of his aftershave. His nails were perfectly manicured; no scuff marks marred his glossy black shoes.

I had to force myself to concentrate on Lou's words as Lucinda spoke them, instead of on the evaluation this stranger would soon reveal to all of New York and beyond. Though I sat at the end of a row of seats, I knew Lou wouldn't creep close to touch me, not with the critic to my other side. Each time the reviewer moved a foot or hand or slightly adjusted his seating, almost sensing the pressure of my anxiety, I felt him changing my position as well. He was manipulating my future as if it were on strings.

All around me people seemed to be simultaneously practicing their nervous tics and glancing the critic's way. And while something was terribly wrong with such reverence for one opinion, a *Times* review was undeniably powerful. If an unfavorable review was published, some of the actors were sure to quit before the end of the show's run. All the people involved in the production, including Lou, would begin to doubt their judgment. On the other hand, a positive review could catapult these same people toward recognition and more plays, movies, television. The show might move to a larger theater with a larger audience.

Although I'd had a couple of adjectives applied to my name at different points in my career — satisfying . . . capable . . . amusing — I'd generally been overlooked as an actor. Comments on Lou's work, however, had been more pointed. An out-of-town paper had described one of his plays as "about as subtle as a bag of cow chips dropped from a tenth-floor window". I'd never understood why the writer decided on the tenth floor or why cow chips would have been in a building to begin with.

Sometimes worse than a negative review itself was the aftermath — the phone calls from friends and enemies, the condolences as if someone had died, the reminders that you were still one of them, struggling for recognition. Stunned with the news of your own unsuccess, it was impossible to determine any caller's actual motive.

Suddenly I sensed the reviewer beside me smiling, signaling slight approval of some particular line or action. I had to resist grabbing him, kissing both his cheeks. At the curtain call, he clapped courteously but with restraint. Someone in the back of the theater let go an embarrassingly long whistle and someone else yelled "Bravo". Although I sensed that the audience had genuinely enjoyed the play, those final exclamations sounded applied by overreacting friends. I envisioned Lou with his head in his hands.

Exhausted, I trailed the reviewer out into the lobby. He nodded politely or spoke briefly with a few people but guarded his opinion like a winning Lotto ticket. Each obligatory phrase he uttered ended with a slight question mark, as if he wanted no one to anticipate his true reaction to any part of the play. As he slipped into his dark overcoat and then out into the darker night, I wanted to call to him, "Tell them. Tell them all."

Tell them it was wonderful.

The normally unapproachable Lucinda tapped me lightly. "Renata, did he laugh?" Her eyes were wide; her breath reeked of cigarettes. She spoke quickly. "I thought we were OK tonight, didn't you?"

"You were great," I said, though I'd hardly caught one full line.

"IT WON'T BE IN the paper already," I said when Lou eased out of bed at six o'clock the next morning. But there would be no reasoning with him until the review appeared in print; he would remain irritable and moody, his usual nonchalance displaced by outbursts of anxiety. From past experience, I could predict his pre-review state of mind as accurately as progressive cold symptoms.

To go out for the daily papers, he was pulling on the clothes he'd taken off six hours earlier. Lou wanted to read the review before anyone from the theater could call him with the news. As he thumped around the room in the dark, he seemed so much like his father — the construction laborer at daybreak already sunk into the burden of the day's routine.

By the time Lou returned, coffee was ready. As he flipped the paper onto the wooden kitchen table, I smelled lingering cigarette smoke emanating like bad news.

"No review," he said. And I held myself, as I knew I would for the next couple of days, from telling him, "Of course not. Not yet. It's too soon."

Reviews of Broadway openings were usually found in the papers the morning after. But Off- and Off Off-Broadway reviews were less predictable, less immediate.

Even as I spoke of coffee, I wasn't thinking of the warming liquid and I knew Lou wasn't either. Both of us were considering a situation we no longer discussed: A friend who wrote amazing plays and a critic who wrote devastating reviews of each one as if his mission were to squelch a voice that might outlive him. Finally, the friend stopped writing plays and turned to teaching. We remembered our friend whenever we proclaimed that true talent would win out over narrow-minded criticism.

"Do you think what Nember said was a sign?" Lou finally asked. He had offered a secondary role to Todd Nember who'd refused because he said he couldn't "afford another bad review".

"Nember's an idiot. A self-serving, egotistical idiot."

When I put my arms around Lou, something felt different, hard and out of place. I pulled back and touched the breast pocket of his blue chamois shirt. Lou lifted his hands in a gesture of surrender; I'd found him out. Hidden in the dark fold of cloth lay a small, plastic likeness of the Sacred Heart.

"All actors are egotistical," he said, seeming to forget that I, too, was among those ranks. We just looked at each other over cups of coffee that had already cooled.

"MAYBE THEY AREN'T going to run it," Lou said a week later. We were soaking in the bathtub in water as hot as was bearable. Besides the bed, it was the largest piece of "furniture" in our apartment and our daily place of discussion. "It's never taken this long."

"Of course they'll run it." My words came slow and determined into the steamy room. "Why don't we go to the show tonight?"

"Not a good idea," he said, explaining that the director said the production was fine, the house nearly full since opening. Lou worried that his appearance at the theater now would somehow be bad luck.

"Ren, I want you to do something for me."

"What's that?"

"Shave."

By the slinky way that he spoke the word, I knew he wasn't talking about a few routine swipes of the razor along my legs. He meant something more, something bizarre.

"I'll do it, too," he said.

"What *exactly* are we talking about?"

He said that we should remove the covering to our most private spots, lay bare our vulnerability, become almost childlike. I told him he was going too far, but even as I argued he enticed me. He spoke so softly, so urgently, touched the razor so tenderly to my mass of darkness, that I allowed him. With short, determined strokes he followed the delicately fleshy curves until only a few traces of hair remained. Then he shaved those as well. I watched as he did the same to himself, though hardly with as much care. Our sexual designations looked new and obvious.

"Let's keep going." I felt his words on my sleek body. Tufts of pubic hair floated all around us.

"What *exactly* do you mean?"

Lou pointed to my head, the dark reddish drift that for the past ten years had reached the middle of my back.

For a minute, I was terrified that he would seduce me beyond all rationality. "Why don't we see how this works first?" I offered, pointing to my groin.

Instead of arguing, Lou turned on himself, on what he'd reduced himself to. "They write these reviews as if

you'd purposely set out to insult them." Lou pulled himself up out of the water. Tiny curls and lines of hairs were
stuck all over his body like commas and parts of letters —
a review that hadn't yet come into focus. "The tone these
guys use is always, 'How dare you, you untalented dick'."
He looked down at me. "What did I ever do to them?"

FOR THE NEXT THREE DAYS we didn't mention reviews.
Without further complaint, Lou got up to buy the paper
as routinely as a subway worker on the early shift. He returned without it when he found no review.

The review grew into a barrier between us. I even
considered whether Lou's play was really good or if we
both wanted so desperately for it to be good that we'd
come to believe in a lie. Soaking in the tub with him each
late afternoon until the steamy water cooled was one ritual
we held to in spite of our emotional disruption.

Otherwise we said little to each other. Lou's silence,
his physical reserve, developed into a new ceremony of
reverence for the unspoken word. When I became most
impatient with him, I thought him an impenetrable nui-
sance. But other times, I imagined he was attempting to
make a magic charm of himself.

THE STAGE MANAGER called Lou. The conversation from
his end was not the normal string of jokes and gossip but a
series of grunts and OKs.

"What?" I asked as soon as he'd hung up.

"The *Times* called the theater and asked for a photo
from the play." As if reading my thoughts, he said, "Don't
be suckered in. I've seen them run a picture — a good-
sized picture — from a play they'd just blown to smithereens."

"Smithereens?"

"You know what I mean. These guys use grenades."

I wasn't sure Lou was right. He'd been anticipating only the worst, negative adjectives that rhymed with the title of his play, headlines that made a pun of his years of work, phrases reducing what he wrote to a joke. I indulged his pessimism but I couldn't help considering the opposite. If a bad review could at best hold you in place, at worst relegate you to a lower order, couldn't a paragraph of praise have some equivalent power? Maybe both of us were as afraid of moving ahead as of returning to what we knew all too well.

In a good review, the audience never stops applauding. The clash of flesh on flesh follows you home and continues until you fall asleep, and still stings with approval when you wake. You can't stop it. Everyone you've ever known hears the clapping. It surrounds you, holds you tightly until all hunger disappears. It ends momentarily only to extend a hand upward toward a gilded room where everyone is smiling. The whole time you are there among the chosen, you say, to no one in particular, "I must be dreaming. I could not have made this happen to myself."

DAYS OF WORK and auditions and meals moved by as if I were living a part written specifically for me. I felt, especially when I touched newsprint, that someone had already figured out the plot of my life and I had simply to speak its lines. I'd felt the same a couple of years earlier when cancer was discovered in my best friend's body. Drifting through whole days speaking phrases so automatic that I seemed to have memorized them, I sensed the outcome of the situation was already known by everyone but was purposely being withheld from me.

At six o'clock on Friday morning, before Lou got out of bed, he said, "I don't know how much longer I can take this."

"I'll go," I offered, slipping into a coat without even brushing my teeth.

The morning was crisp and too bright. I squinted walking to the corner of the nearly deserted street. If I yelled, my voice would blow right back against my teeth. I selected a newspaper from the middle of the pile as if choosing one playing card from a deck, then held it carefully, not wanting to disturb any possible good luck.

A couple of homeless men were still asleep in a pharmacy doorway. One of the men stretched and stood up as I walked by. He was wearing someone's discarded tuxedo. Over a white shirt, the black coat was rumpled and one of the pockets torn. The man dug into the torn pocket probably for a cigarette or a coin he'd forgotten about, some reason to start the day.

I suddenly wondered what had possessed Lou and me to get involved in the theater. No one in either of our families had an interest in the arts. They were too busy working or getting ready for work or sleeping off the exhaustion that work had pressed onto them. And yet, even though I understood that we'd stepped outside our element, I knew it was too late. We'd invested too many years in the theater to ever give it up willingly.

Farther down the block a church announced its intentions with a pronounced steeple pointing skyward. Everything I looked at appeared too clear, too sharply in focus. Only after I sat on the steps of the church did I open the paper. Looking over the articles on the front page, I wanted to remember this day as the one on which my husband was rewarded, the day on which he finally gained some respect from his family of devout nine-to-fivers. Even our neighbor Lester had gotten payback for his prior good deeds.

I glanced at the index for the Arts section but refrained from hurrying. Instead, I progressed slowly through one section of the paper, started anew with the next. The longer I studied articles on highway accidents and political repressions in Africa and scientific replacement of body parts, the less significant a single theater review seemed. Maybe the relationship that Lou and I had was the extent of our fortune. Maybe bathed together in tenderness, we could never truly face brutality. But the closer I came to the Arts section, the more my anxiety grew. The ramifications of acceptance or rejection felt more crucial than ever.

I would be the one to tell him. My heart began to beat faster as I reached the pages of arts-related articles. I scanned music and dance news in my search for theater. Bodies paired with success as well as failure were flung throughout the black-and-white pages. Reading and rereading the headlines, I came up with nothing familiar. I continued skimming the paper in the off-chance that the review had slid even deeper into the vat of news. I reread the arts pages. After digesting a negative film review, I remembered an argument about criticism that I'd had with Lou. "Get it straight, Ren," he'd said. "Critics are consumer advocates these days. Most of them don't even like films."

"I thought you'd hung yourself," Lou said when I finally returned to the apartment. "Where were you?" He grabbed the paper with the desperation of a fugitive. I just shook my head.

"No?" He looked at the paper, then back at me. "No, it's not in here, or no, it's no good?"

"There's no review today."

"Shit."

His eyes were heavy from over two weeks of intermittent sleep. "I'll settle for them calling it offbeat," he said.

"Don't settle for anything." The husband who normally met the world on his own terms was whimpering behind the scenes. I reminded myself that his condition was temporary.

"Just not 'forgettable,' " he said, once again going through a string of possible headlines. "Just not a reprimand like, 'Why don't you quit this playwriting and go back to cleaning public toilets'."

He put his arm around me as the coffee dripped beside us. "What I hate most of all," he said into my hair, "is when they turn your characters' words against you."

"They try to be witty."

That night, in his sleep, Lou said distinctly, "They're going to call me a woman-hater."

Without hesitation, I woke him before his worry could turn into a nightmare. "Who would call you that?"

"Huh?"

"Lou, you were talking in your sleep. Why do you think that someone would call you a woman-hater?"

"I said that?" He paused and then said sleepily, "Because it's a fashionable thing to say?"

Even in the haze of just waking, I envisioned countless malicious faces, huge fingers pressing the keys of the alphabet into a pattern of lies.

"Maybe people without a sense of humor will fry me," he said.

"Nobody's going to fry you." I spoke softly, though I couldn't be sure of that promise. These days there were so many striking agendas that gained more prominence than the truth.

While I waited to fall back into sleep, I went over my theory that comedy puts everyone on equal footing during the seconds it takes to laugh, but that some people always want to stand apart — or above — no matter how funny something really is.

ON TUESDAY of that week, we went back to *Ever More* so Lou could see how the actors were holding up with the weighty analysis of their accomplishment still a secret.

During intermission, various people patted him on the back or squeezed his hand in support but they didn't say much. In the fuzzy air, I sensed that the tentative camaraderie would last only until a single critical statement was issued. Then the other actors could gather around to pick and pick until a gaping hole took the place of collaboration.

When the show was over, everyone involved hung around backstage. No one mentioned hurrying off to a party or reading another script or having a sick roommate. Just as Lou sent a great smoke ring into the air above my head the way he'd done when we met, the stage manager ran toward him with a newspaper. The room went as silent, as still, as just after a gun is fired.

A true professional, the stage manager gave no clue as to the review's contents. All that she would reveal was that she'd snuck off to the *Times* building as she had almost every night since the reviewer's appearance. Lou took the paper, folded it over to the article that could touch everyone in the room. A large photo of Lucinda was planted to the side of the review. The flimsy paper shook in Lou's hands as he read. I closed my eyes, allowing him the privilege of reading the review first.

"Out loud," someone called.

Lou looked up briefly and said simply, "No." Then everyone seemed to hold his breath. As he read, I told myself that no one in the room wanted more from life than the average worker. They simply wanted to be admired for their talent, their special ability. But if I were honest about these actors and even Lou, I knew no review was capable of fulfilling their needs.

Lou took a deep breath in the silence. I heard his

familiar voice return. "I'll take it." He was smiling. Instantly, the veil of fear and apprehension and physical, flulike symptoms was thrown off.

"Take it?" the stage manager asked. He handed the paper to her, permission for her to cut loose. "It's great!" she yelled.

The others gathered around her, pressed and groped and strained with hunger for their share of the good news. Someone screamed; someone else made a noise as if air were being squeaked out of a balloon. Lucinda lay flat on the bare floor; she was chain-smoking and running her fingers through her hair, again. Someone was suggesting places they might all go for a celebratory drink. The room that had been soundless with fear minutes earlier was now alive with laughter and one voice reading aloud key complimentary phrases. Actors, tech people, the director, Lou, clapped and congratulated one another.

I hugged Lou before I got the review to myself. His arms were taut. "Something paid off," he whispered to me at the exact instant that I was trying to pinpoint which of his incantations had worked. Would they *all* have to be repeated, along with a couple of new ones, next time? Tickly hair was already growing back from my shaving incident. I hung back as Lou moved toward the others, toward a tight, bright circle of praise lit by meager backstage lights, where momentarily the happiness in our newsprint-stained hands went beyond the review, beyond the stage, beyond any preconception of success.

4

The First Time

The first time Ren and Lou flew from New York to Los Angeles they were overloaded with hope and, although they'd been married nearly ten years, still encumbered by a certain innocence. The trip, Lou reminded Renata, was speculative. Ren and Lou knew how to live with risk. Hadn't they decided to marry within days of meeting each other? Weren't they both in the theater?

An enthusiastic assessment of Lou's one-act *Fortunes*, coupled with the earlier review of *Ever More*, had enticed a movie producer to invite him to a party. When the first-class airline ticket in addition to accommodations at a deluxe hotel arrived in the mail, Lou explained, "They want to check me out." He paused. "They want to schmooze is all." Producers, Lou surmised, were not quick to make commitments.

Lou's recently acquired agent, a slight, pouty man with a mass of curly hair, suggested that Lou go out to L.A. a couple of days prior to the party for appointments he would make with various other producers.

"Already I feel like a whore," Lou said.

He insisted that Ren accompany him because the day he was scheduled to return home was their anniversary. "I have to pay for a hotel for three nights anyway. You might as well come," he said.

"What about my airline ticket?" Ren asked, visualizing the transaction on their Visa bill along with the already-accumulated debt.

"We'll worry about that when we get back," he said.

Ren suggested that for the cost of the First-Class airfare, they could have paid for two coach round-trips to L.A., as well as meals and other expenses. Ren knew about money. In reply to her concern, Lou said, "That's not the way they do it in Hollywood. Out there it's a whole different ball game." He explained that lavishness was more valued than practicality. The carriage of success attracted success; on the west coast appearances were crucial. Lou was so superstitious about what he called his "first crack at Hollywood" that he didn't examine the first-class ticket more than once or twice a day.

IN TEN YEARS, Ren had tried to conquer her tendency toward flightiness, while becoming firm in her dedication to her own role in the theater. She imagined her single-mindedness made a clear strong path through her body the way her legs had tightened from routine exercising. But nothing spectacular had happened yet.

From her aisle seat in coach, Ren could catch a glimpse of Lou's forearm, part of his shoulder, part of his head. The flight attendant in First Class was pouring champagne and delivering glasses of sparkling liquid to each passenger before she pulled a curtain across the archway separating the seats of privilege from the masses.

Ren reflected that for years she had thought she would be the family success. Her theory that there might only be so much creativity and good luck between them caused her to imagine being discovered during one of the showcase productions she'd acted in at warehouses and restaurants, church balconies, and the front half of strangers' loft apartments. Once she'd gotten a rave review for her performance in *Miss Julie,* when Lou's play running at the same time hadn't even been acknowledged. She'd fantasized lifting the two of them from their dank, cramped basement apartment toward the shocking light of recognition, of success.

During one of her daydreams at a temp job for two self-important divorce attorneys, Ren's hands were noticed as she worked a copier, which jammed routinely. A movie director, who was in the office to discuss his settlement, said Ren would be fantastic in the role of a deaf-mute pianist, who played so beautifully that she could make people weep. Tragically, she couldn't hear herself and that irony would seduce people to cry as well.

To avoid the possibility of their marriage becoming an artistic battleground, Ren never appeared, in fact, never even envisioned herself, in one of Lou's plays. Still, if she ran into an agent on the street in Hollywood, it couldn't hurt if she showed the news clips critiquing her past performances.

Thirty minutes later when a flight attendant finally reached Ren's row with the drink cart, Ren said, "I'll have champagne." The drink set her back $3.50. It wasn't graciously poured, patiently attended to as the bubbles settled down, and then carefully repoured to a proper level as she'd seen Lou receive his. A twist-off green bottle smaller than a wine cooler was set before her; an upturned plastic cup swayed against the bottle neck.

By the time Ren drained the bottle she was missing Lou, though he was only a patterned blue curtain away. She was annoyed at the large man seated beside her who continually opened and closed a briefcase full of toys and games, candy and gum, and popular magazines. In the brief conversation in which they identified themselves, he as a manufacturer of chemical gases, he asked Ren, "Have I seen anything you were in?"

Ren stood up, and although she could feel the champagne tickling her emotions, she boldly walked past the First-Class boundary and approached Lou.

"Hey," he said, immediately moving over to the empty adjoining seat to make room.

"Want to hang in for the movie?" he asked and winked. "They don't charge for headsets up here." Ren studied Lou's dark hair, his darker eyes, his casual, khaki-colored shirt that didn't easily identify him. Lou's prospects, she had to admit, looked even better in his large seat.

"Excuse me," the flight attendant said loudly to her.

"It's all right. This is my wife," Lou said.

"Could I see your ticket?" the attendant asked.

As the attendant held onto a seat to steady herself in the turbulence, Ren felt like asking the woman if the horseshoe earrings she was wearing weren't in violation of the airline's dress code. Instead, she confessed, "My seat's in the other section."

Then Lou said, "Aw, give us a break for a few minutes," and gently put his hand on Ren's thigh. Lou was normally a cautious man but he tossed off his moderation as if it were a shirt he'd decided not to wear.

"I'm afraid this isn't Yankee Stadium," the attendant replied without looking at either of them. "You can't just move up." While she began to explain about ticket restrictions, a second attendant, younger and blonde, appeared.

"What d'y'all have, a fight or something?" the blonde asked as she looked from Ren to Lou and then back to Ren.

"I'm afraid . . ." the one with the horseshoe earrings started again. But Ren was gone, her role played out, before the words squeezed past the attendant's deep red lips.

EVEN BEFORE REN visited a city, it existed in her mind as a symbol on a map. Paris was a golden, plastic Eiffel Tower; Orlando, a gray, smiling dolphin jumping through a hoop; Las Vegas, a steel-toed cowboy bent over a slot machine. And Hollywood was a black clapboard marked with the sharply lettered directive "Take One". Behind the snap of the clapboard, beyond the call for silence, Ren saw a TV scene of a congenial special family seated around a large kitchen table designed for togetherness and long, comfortable indulgences with food.

The actual strip of Hollywood Boulevard, near the hotel where Ren and Lou had prepaid reservations, suggested anything but families. The shop windows featured leather, three-for-six-dollars T-shirts, and lingerie in black and blue and purple. The littered and gum-pocked sidewalks were populated by women wearing stretch tops, hot pants and metallic necklaces; earrings and bracelets were jingling and dangling as if something essential in them were broken and might at any moment fall off.

In Ren and Lou's life together, they'd seen despair; they'd witnessed friends abandon their dreams; they'd watched their grandparents grow old and ignored until their worlds became small as cedar chests. But Ren had never before seen such a magnitude of failure concentrated in one place — its devastation strewn across whole faces and blocks of buildings. Defeat was evident in the buildings and people, both carefully patched or prettied up with extraneous accessories.

Ren held tightly to Lou's hand and hoped that the neighborhood would suddenly shift, as it often had when they'd lived in Brooklyn, from a seedy enclosure of poverty to a block of stone and wood rubbed clean of abuses. But before they found a suitable place to eat, Ren and Lou stood at the front door to the May Hotel, hardly the "quaint and welcoming sight" described in the budget guidebook.

To the right of the registration area was a glassed-in common room with a television at its core. The guests were disheveled and loud and the majority of them seemed to be abusing one substance or another, as well as themselves, in plain view of the evening manager, who introduced himself as Mr. Twick. Parted just above his left ear, Mr. Twick's hair was swept up and over the top of his otherwise-bald head. His teeth were small and very white; his eyes darted like a bird's.

Ren and Lou said nothing as they took the elevator to the sixth floor, which the guidebook had suggested for its nicely furnished kitchenettes. Lou unlocked the metal door, gave it two hard pushes, a kick, and stood back.

"Funky," he said, after quickly looking the place over. He ran his fingers through his hair and searched Ren's face for a reaction.

"You're close," Ren said. "Filthy." The bathroom walls were painted a bumpy maroon. Despite a protective paper seal crossing the toilet, a substance resembling oatmeal floated on the water's surface. The miniature, inoperative refrigerator gave off an odor of rotten chicken. Ren dropped onto the double bed, raised only slightly off the discolored shag rug. A large corner of the nubby, navy-blue bedspread was stained and wet.

From the greasy window, its venetian blind permanently askew and raised halfway, Ren spotted their view of Hollywood — seven black plastic trash bags pitched onto the roof of the adjoining building. The bags had split open either from the force of their landing or the efforts of hungry creatures.

"Let's go get a drink," Lou said.

THEY ORDERED EGGS BENEDICT, the most affordable item on the menu, and Jack Daniel's straight up.

Lou said, "That place is not going to look as bad when we get back."

Ren wanted to believe him, but she knew that certain facts wouldn't change no matter how many drinks they had. And at this place, they couldn't afford many.

From the waiter's surly manner, Ren figured that many years earlier he had arrived in Los Angeles with other aspirations tucked into his luggage. After their second drinks Lou said, "It'll be all right." He placed his hands over Ren's. "Three nights and then we move to the fancy hotel that's on Neville Morris."

Assuring and reassuring through all monetary and artistic obstacles was Ren's job. Usually she was persuaded by her own voice when repeating her faith in their artistic goals. But this night as Lou attempted to steer her back to the safety that marriage had made for them, she was immobile, almost in shock.

"We'll get a kick out of this in a couple of weeks," he offered next. But he looked frightened and a little too animated. Lou had one more drink, and as much as Ren fought her inclination to cry, it overcame her. "We'll get another place," Lou said quickly. Ren shook her head. As she thought of Mr. Twick refunding their money, she began to laugh.

DURING THE DAYS when Lou was escorted to different movie studios, introduced to industry personalities, probed for story ideas, and fed at chic eateries, Ren fled the May Hotel and walked around Los Angeles. She quickly discovered that walking in the city was not a preferred way of moving unless you were crazy or homeless. And not even a crazy person walked the distances, at the pace, that Ren walked, her arms in stiff synchronization with her long strides.

She temporarily forgot about contracts and agents and verbal agreements, and walked off her anxiety and the thick air of the May Hotel, which clung to her hair and clothes like smoke. She strode beyond her own ambitions. For hours as she walked, she imagined she was solidifying her bond with Lou.

THURSDAY AFTERNOON REN and Lou moved to the hotel that the producer, Neville Morris, had reserved. The spacious lobby, its every surface polished to a high sheen, made Ren worry that her suitcase might hold a few crawling remnants of the May Hotel.

"My God," Lou said when they unlocked the door on a living room area that led, in one direction, onto a private balcony, and, in the other, into a bedroom featuring a king-sized bed. A basket of fresh fruit sat on a table next to a refrigerator stocked with drinks and snacks.

"There's three phones in this place," Ren said. "Even one next to the toilet," she added as she filled the sparkling marble tub with hot water and prepared to soak.

Ren and Lou drove a rented Toyota to the party at Neville Morris's home. Here success was flaunted as overtly as desperation at the May Hotel. Bel Air's streets and homes made her avert her eyes, almost in embarrassment. The lush lawns and flowered walkways, manicured palm trees, the delicately detailed, yet impenetrable, gateways demanded respectful sidelong glances and silence. A lone bird twittered with perfectly spaced pauses as Ren and Lou walked toward their destination. Nothing was out of place, except for their rental car parked between a Mercedes and a Jaguar. A handsome guy at the Morris's gate handed them a pale-green parking sign to place inside the Toyota so that its presence would not be questioned.

For Ren, "home" did not seem to be the appropriate designation for a place so starkly modern, so huge, so perfectly furnished and decorated that one room ran smoothly into the next as if extravagance were ordinary. Her footsteps echoed briefly across the courtyard where the air suddenly became so heavy and musky with vegetation that she thought of a swift, passionate encounter. On the terrace, waiters dressed in stiff, black-and-white uniforms offered wine or sparkling water, cheeses, and vegetables cut into the shape of lilies. The servers, all young, all beautiful, spoke in nods or hushed educated tones. "Wow," she heard Lou say softly.

Ren felt a debilitating sadness overcome her. A whole class of dreamers who had come to L.A. as promising actors and screenwriters now made their living parking other people's cars, serving them dinner, monitoring their pools and lawns.

Ren and Lou were introduced around by Neville who maintained a continual, almost manic, enthusiasm. Ren smiled proudly at the adjectives that gathered around Lou's name — "promising," "talented," "delightful. . . ." A few people asked what Ren did, and when she replied that she was an actor, they smiled as though this was something that few admitted in public.

Ren began to notice that, with the exception of a drunken actor who affected an Irish brogue, people seemed not to focus on her, but mostly looked over her shoulder to the person they could speak to next. The habit reminded Ren of unskilled actors who didn't truly hear the lines preceding and following their own. She realized she wasn't someone who could be of use to anyone here. She was someone in need — no, worse — an appendage of someone in need.

A small young woman asked Ren, "Your eyes aren't natural, are they?"

Ren could only stare at her and accept what followed as a compliment: "I've never seen eyes such a brilliant shade of blue." Then, without mentioning her name or asking Ren's, the woman drifted off.

As Ren walked to the bathroom the hostess, Sally Morris, a fleshy, elegant woman in a navy-blue silk pants outfit, put her arm around Ren.

"Darling," she said, "your husband is such a prize."

Ren saw Lou being toted by Neville Morris through the party conversations like a huge just-caught fish.

"I guess I'll keep him for a while," Ren said and smiled.

Sally Morris squeezed Ren's hand very hard and pulled her in. Her perfume made Ren dizzy. Her painstakingly curled hair was as unexpectedly soft as a small animal's fur. Ren held onto the large, warm hand after Mrs. Morris had dropped it to her side.

Ren spotted Lou, flanked by two fortyish men and a young woman. Something Lou said made the men laugh and the young woman move in closer. One of the men loudly told Lou he should relocate to Los Angeles. He mentioned the weather, the good roads, the excellent food, the writing opportunities as plentiful as oranges.

"My wife," Lou started to say. He frequently used Ren as his excuse when he was unsure or unconvinced of some idea or another.

"Well, we'll just get you a wife out here," one of the men said and laughed. For a minute, Ren couldn't hear anybody say anything. Finally she felt Lou's eyes on her as she stood next to a fountain, its unnatural spray breaking the water's glossy blue surface.

THEY DROVE OFF from the well-guarded stretches of greenery and back to the hotel a little drunk. She tried to explain how at the party she'd felt caught in a huge cliché, yet, at the same time, everything had appeared new and original. Was that because the clichés were happening to her? The way that Lou drove without mentioning the proposal to move to L.A., and without either of them noticing the road other than to assume they were driving in the right general direction, made Ren think of those adolescent days just before sex. Those long hours when everywhere was dark and musty, her mouth had tasted of too-many cigarettes and not enough alcohol, and the possibility existed of saying yes to the dangerously attractive decision. Boy lips were soft but behind them was an urgency that made her close her eyes. Yet beneath her apprehension, she knew it was her decision to stop things. The girl's decision made the difference.

Ren had mistakenly thought back then, as surely as she hoped now, that such a crucial choice would deliver her from the agitation of indecision, make her embrace an identity of some kind. But a yes to Hollywood like a yes to sex would probably mean things would only become more complicated, not more defined.

And yet, this decision was no longer in her hands. Because Lou had been the one discovered and courted by Hollywood, he should be the one to determine how their lives would change. If things worked out for him, if their lives suddenly became easier, maybe he'd no longer need a marriage that was founded on struggle. Success could, without warning, suddenly knock your metabolism out of synch, make you feel you were getting sick.

THE NEXT MORNING when Ren and Lou slipped out from under the crisp percale sheets and left the hotel, the air was damp and slightly cool. Unlike the cab drivers in New York who rushed to destinations as if they were meeting a deadline, the L.A. cabbie drove the wide morning-lit streets with unhurried calm. He didn't stop talking except to ask where they were from, and then he reported New York's weather like the radio.

She daydreamed while Lou made polite noises to indicate that he heard the driver's stories about different Hollywood murders and was interested in the sites of several gruesome crimes along the way. As Ren anticipated the flight home, the names of movie stars from one of the cabbie's recitations snuck into her thoughts. The last thing he said as he deposited them at the airport was, "What am I going on about crimes for? You're from New York, right?"

"In New York we expect it," Lou said. He insisted on handling the check-in at the ticket counter, not the usual way they worked; ordinarily Ren took care of details — money, checks, appointments, tickets. She felt a little uneasy with the new arrangement.

At the gate they drank coffee and didn't say much. When Ren boarded behind Lou, he stopped her in First Class.

"Sit here," Lou said, indicating a seat next to him.

"I don't know, Lou." She scanned the aisles for a stiff attendant wearing horseshoe earrings. But Ren sat beside Lou and studied each passenger coming down the aisle, forging straight ahead, wheeling carry-on luggage too big for the overhead bins. No one looked at Ren or checked a piece of paper and said, "I'm afraid you have my seat."

"Looks like the plane's going to be pretty full," Lou said.

"I'd better go back. Let me have my ticket."

"Stay," he said. Lou took her bag and slid it beneath the seat in front of him just as the engines fired up. The flight attendant gave no sign that Ren was out of place.

"Lou," Ren said loudly. The plane had begun to taxi down the runway.

"This is your seat," he said as the plane paused at the

end of the next runway, straining to break from the ground.

"What do you mean?"

"Happy Anniversary."

"Lou, the money . . ." she said, the plane's take-off covering her words. Lou put his finger to her lips. Ren looked behind, toward coach class, and wondered if he were holding something from her. But his only explanation for adding this expense to their dark lines of debt was, "We've always gambled."

A few minutes later the plane leveled off and the seat belt lights above Ren and Lou's heads went out. The 757 cut through masses of white clouds. Ren had the sense that she and Lou were on their way somewhere entirely new, a place for which she had no clichéd icon stored in her imagination. It was a quarter to twelve. At her side a young blonde attendant smiled and held an open bottle. "Champagne?" she asked, and waited for Ren to decide.

5
New House

On Friday morning the dull green Pontiac Bonneville pulled into Ren and Lou's driveway. Ren watched from the upstairs window as her mother and father and brother and sister-in-law popped out of the rusting car like springs that had been compressed for too long a time. One of the car doors made a deep groan when it opened and another replicated a loud yelp before it slammed shut.

Beyond a hedge of forsythia in full bloom, Ren's family stretched and looked over the Connecticut property that she and Lou had bought two months earlier.

"They're here," Ren called to Lou in the shower.

"I thought they had a six-hour trip. When the hell could they have left?"

She heard the soap hit the porcelain as it slipped from her husband's hands.

REN'S MOTHER wore a large, pale-yellow short-sleeved dress, which Ren had never seen before, and held a cigarette in her hand, extended as if she were taking an oath. Careful not to jostle the long, tenuous ash, Ren hugged her mother. Next she squeezed her much smaller father, who, as usual, was dressed from hat to shoes in varying shades of brown.

"Where are all these deer we've been hearing so much about, Renata?" Ren's mother asked, smoke coming out with her words.

"Oh, we're sure to see a few before the weekend's over," Ren assured them. As she pointed out the boundaries of the property and the outline of stone wall visible from where they stood, Ren noticed David's wife Lilly teetering on three-inch red heels that had sunk into the newly laid, crushed stone driveway.

"Hey," David said and kissed Ren on the forehead. Ren and her brother, who was two years older, had reddish hair and blue eyes, and whenever she saw him she felt the same familiar comfort as looking into a mirror.

"When I was a young man, I ran into a poor little deer. Over on Greenspring Avenue," Ren's father said, looking down at his tan shoes losing their luster as he swiped one, then the other, back and forth across the stone and dirt.

"That was a dog," Ren's mother said flatly.

"How the hell do you know, Nella? I wasn't even married to you yet."

"I know," she said and lit another cigarette. "It was a golden retriever."

As she had all of her life, Ren directed her family out of an argument and toward another distraction—her home, the house in the country she'd never truly believed she would own as she and Lou moved from one small apartment to another, at each transition holding onto the blueprints she'd sketched long ago. When Lou's play, *Blue Corners,* sold to the movies, they were delivered from those basement rooms, walk-up apartments, and studios in "lively" neighborhoods to this spacious wooded place. The flower gardens were colored with sprays of lilacs and purple and yellow crocuses, with deep-green leafy promises of peonies and rhododendron.

The days before Ren and Lou settled on points, locked in a rate, received the loan approval, they couldn't sleep. With so much to put down in one spot, Ren thought constantly, will we make it?

After they'd moved to Long Wood, Ren felt she spent whole days walking through the rooms, the echo of her steps on the bare oak floors placing her far from the stress of auditions. She peered into empty closets and out windows at hundreds of trees as if this were an entirely new stage. In Brooklyn, where their third-floor apartment had fronted the Brooklyn-Queens Expressway, they kept their windows closed against fine black dust gathering on the window ledges and the steady growl of traffic that occasionally broke into the screech and crack of an accident. In front of the row house, during Ramadan, their landlord and his extended family, who lived on the main floor, celebrated around a scraggly three-foot bush.

Every so often now, Ren felt she was acting the part of a wealthy, fortunate woman. The concept of owning trees, many of them far older than she was, still seemed as unlikely as possessing the sky above them.

"We made pretty good time," David said. "Ma closed her eyes while we went through New York City."

"I was sleeping," she said, but not even Lilly believed her.

Ren's father said, "She was nervous as a cat."

"I was tired. We left Baltimore at four o'clock in the morning, for God's sake."

Ren thought of her family's two-bedroom Cape in a landscape of identical working-class houses, each with a square of yard bounded by chain-link fence. Within the last three years, white vinyl siding had spread through the neighborhood like a blight, obliterating the different colors. Even so, that small unpretentious house that Ren had grown up in was the first image that came to her when she heard the word "home".

"We left early," David said patiently, "so we would avoid hitting New York City at a bad time." On car trips when Ren and David were kids, her father had used the same logic. Normally an easy-going man, he grew frantic, even reckless, in traffic. And as he aged his panic unfurled into areas other than congested highways.

Now he was disoriented by the new surroundings. He rubbed at his upper lip with the back of his hand. "Whatever made you decide to move way the hell up here, Renata?" As Ren put her arm around him, she felt his small, bony shoulders. She had her father's facial structure, and sometimes she found herself absently rubbing the edge of her ear as he often did.

"Because, Dad, you know we have to be near New York. And it beats living in the city." Ren had to keep reminding her family that she was an actor and her husband a writer. She had been hired for two television commercials in the past six months. And last week she'd done a voice-over for furniture polish.

While she once again explained that she and Lou didn't work in a hospital or a restaurant where they could pick up and put down just anywhere, she heard her own voice sounding as calm and confident as when she'd promoted the long-lasting effects of lemon wax. But even as she spoke, she knew that around family it was impossible to act professional for long.

When they stepped into the living room, its walls covered with dark panels of natural wood, Ren noticed that the thick main beam above their heads stretched across the ceiling in a direct path to Lou. His hair was still wet from the shower. He looked ruddy and strong. Ren thought that if you had to circle one who didn't belong of the six standing there in the living room, like comparison tests she'd taken as a child, you'd have to pick Lou. When she and Lou had first met, they hadn't been able to keep their hands off the exotic other.

"So," Lou said, "how was your trip?" And they all began talking at once.

Ren set up the coffee pot. It was way too early for lunch — an array of favorite cold cuts, a potato salad she'd made herself with plenty of eggs and mayonnaise, and thick, chunky brownies for dessert. As she dipped slices of bread into an egg mixture for French toast, she heard her husband answering questions about New York City. Her family considered it a foreign country and Lou one of its aboriginals.

"Didn't I read somewhere that Manhattan had more muggings last year than all of the rest of the country combined?" Ren's mother's question snaked into the kitchen.

"She's always reading something," Ren's father said, after all these years still attempting to buffer his wife's bluntness.

"Maybe now they'll have a baby," Ren heard her mother say to David.

Since Ren and Lou had been married, they'd been plagued by three questions when they told anyone what they were about — Have you been in anything I might have seen? Have you written anything I might have heard of? Do you have children? They'd learned to answer the first two questions in clever ways that would subtly nip at the inquisitor. Their favorite retort for the third question was, "No, we've been lucky so far."

Ren pretended she hadn't heard her mother's comment and quickly called the family to breakfast.

"DON'T WE HAVE a few things to get out of the car?" Ren's father asked as he wiped his mouth of syrup. Eating seemed to have made him more comfortable.

"Bring in your camera, Davey," Lilly advised. She yawned widely like a child, without covering her mouth. Lilly was fifteen years younger than Ren's brother, who was closing in on forty.

"Yeah," agreed Ren's father, "you never know when we might spot one of the deer."

"David, the two coolers," Ren's mother called. "We'll have to get that stuff into the refrigerator."

"This is a very nice house you have, Renata." She lit a cigarette and studied the walls and ceiling. Ren imagined the smoke her mother exhaled filling in the ceiling cracks and spaces between the strips of wood. Then, as if finding the inconsistency — a task she was committed to — Ren's mother said, "Renata, you never liked pink."

To contrast the stained wood walls and beams, Ren and Lou had selected mauve couches. A large photo in a pink frame brightened one side of the room.

"Well, now I like it," Ren said a little defensively. Though she thought the light color made a feminine claim on the dark and cozy quality of the house, she didn't mention this idea to her mother.

"Pink and orange. You never liked either of those colors."

Ren's mother went on about a pink voile dress she'd made that Ren had "turned her nose up at," until Ren said finally, "I was eleven." Even as Ren spoke, she saw that families held up the past as something to conform to forever.

David came through the front door with his camera bag slung over his shoulder, a cooler through his left arm, and a large object wrapped in crinkly white paper in his arms. He set it down carefully in the middle of the room.

"For the new place," he said and stepped away from the gift as if it might be dangerous. It was a foot-and-a-half taller than the end table.

Ren's father followed David with two full-sized suit-cases, which he plopped on the floor. "What in the hell you got in here, Nella?"

"Lead," she said. "I packed them with lead." She lit another cigarette.

"I can't wait for you to open it," Lilly squealed. "I just love presents." Ren's mother rolled her eyes at her daughter-in-law's enthusiasm.

Before he noticed the gift, Lou spotted the two large suitcases situated between him and Ren. He gave Ren a subtle, questioning look, squinting his eyes ever so slightly, mouthing "how long?" — How long did you say they were staying? I thought this was just a weekend visit.

"Why don't you open it, Ren?" Lou said. Lou had always been suspicious of intentions.

"Go ahead, Lilly," Ren said.

"Really?" the young woman asked. She pulled at the paper eagerly.

Ren saw gray and white, something that looked like an animal's ear, a red nose, a large platter . . . She recognized an animal's face. A cat. Lilly stood back from the four-foot striped cat standing on its hind legs and holding a shallow bowl.

"That's something," Lou finally said.

"It's a birdbath," Lilly explained.

"A lawn ornament," Ren's mother added. "Lorraine down the street made it in her ceramics class and I bought it off her."

"She charged you?" Ren's father asked.

"Of course, she charged me. Only for materials, though."

"Tell them about the turtle," Lilly said. She clasped her hands together. Her fingernails were long and colored the same bright red as her lips.

"Lorraine had a turtle, too. He's so cute. He stands

on his back legs and holds his shell up for the birds to wash in. Now you think about it, Renata. Because if you want the turtle, it's no problem for us to exchange it," Ren's mother said.

"Maybe I should have asked Lorraine if she thought about creating a deer. You know, to attract other deer," she said. She looked at Ren as if hoping this would please her.

At Lilly's insistence, David heaved the birdbath into his arms and carried it across the lawn. From the kitchen window, Ren watched her family quibbling over where it looked best. David was focusing his camera on the monstrous cat, trying to persuade the family to stand beside it while he took a photograph.

"WE'VE GOT YOU BEAT," Ren's mother said, pointing at the forsythia and green-tipped trees. "Baltimore must get spring a good two weeks before Connecticut."

After six hours of the visitors, Ren was already a little irritable but she held her tongue as always.

The six were sitting on the grass in webbed lawn chairs. Ren's mother launched into a discourse of the advantages of a full-sized freezer. As she exposed her belief in "stocking up", she sliced a cheese log she'd brought from Baltimore and passed it around on a plate of crackers.

Ren tilted her head far back and looked into the trees. Spring had touched the Bradford pear trees with tufts of flowers resembling cotton and a mist of green hung on a few beeches. Surrounded and protected, she imagined herself enfolded in giant hairs, the tulipwood and maple and ash and oak and evergreen branches all screening the curiosities of her neighbors.

Baltimore life had been far from four-acre zoning. Her parents' house was so close to its neighbor you could smell breakfasts and dinners cooking and hear loud belches at meal times. On the other side of the house, she could actually see Mr. Holt's television from the kitchen window. Most of the time she'd lived in Baltimore she'd stayed deep in her room, shades drawn on the brightest day, dreaming of getting out, escaping scrutiny.

"Renata," her mother said. "Still drifting off when someone's talking to you." Ren had been accused of that fault since she'd learned to tie her own shoes.

"I asked you what your neighbors are like."

"I don't know. I haven't met them," Ren said.

Ren's mother and father stared at her the way they had when she'd announced her decision to marry an Italian from Staten Island without being introduced to his parents. Yet they hadn't put up too much of a fight about the wedding, perhaps hoping marriage would settle her down.

"I can't understand living next to somebody and not knowing who they are," Ren's father said, reaching his right hand across his face to scratch at his left ear.

"We don't know that woman on the second floor, Davey," Lilly said.

"That's because she's a schizophrenic," David said and patted his wife's hand, which was searching out four-leaf clovers.

"We like the privacy," Lou said and shrugged. "That's why we moved here."

"That and they keep promising to repeal the income tax," Ren added. But Ren's mother wasn't going for the diversion.

"Call me crazy, but I have neighbors I can count on, even in the middle of the night," Ren's mother said, her eyebrows up at a sharp angle. She had prepared all her life for the emergency that had never materialized.

"We have 911," Lou said and smiled.

"What if your telephone's out?" Ren's mother persisted. She accepted Lou a little more now that he'd written a movie, soon to be released, and had a new house as an emblem of his success.

Lou threw up his hands and walked off toward the front of the house where the birdbath cat stood out as a reminder of his childhood, too. He had never found comfort in the endless rows of houses with statuary, usually religious, displayed in every other front yard. Both of them preferred the haphazard stretches of trees.

Ren's mother said, "They're not niggers, are they?" Ren stared at her mother without speaking. "Your neighbors. They're not niggers, are they?"

"Last week, Lou and I saw twelve deer under the crab apple tree over there," Ren said finally, taking a hearty swig of vodka and tonic. She thought of all the years at the little tan house in Baltimore, trying to keep the peace by changing the subject, protecting herself.

"You're kidding," Lilly said, then blew a huge bubble of purple gum. Ren could smell the synthetic grape flavor.

Ren was somehow ashamed of her compulsion to show her family proof of the wildlife in much the same way that she'd once tried to justify her career in the theater. Her family had never seen her on stage but she dutifully sent home playbills and favorable reviews.

"Thirteen," Lou said simply. His voice sounded disappointed.

"All I'm asking for is one," David said, not looking away from the lens of his camera.

"*I* FEEL LIKE the damn visitor," Lou said. He lay on his back on a blow-up mattress in an empty room with Ren.

"I know. But it's just for one more night," she said.

The bed was a prop for his real feelings, his lack of faith in himself and his own discomfort as a son and a brother.

"Can you picture my parents on this thing?" Ren asked. She giggled, mostly out of nervousness. "Besides, my father needs to be near the bathroom."

The night after Ren and Lou had moved into their house, the moon had been full and moonlight spilled across the unpacked boxes of clothes in the bedroom. Lou confessed that he was proud to have broken out of the tradition of factory and construction workers and to have been able to make a down payment on a house in the country. When his father died in a construction accident, Lou had been enraged that his life had ended on the job, instead of on the vacation in Florida he had been saving for in secret. Lou felt the company had swallowed his father live.

"I refuse to work my butt off for some cold-ass corporation that doesn't give a damn," he'd said.

When Lou turned on his side, the movement bobbled her into him. She waited for the puffs of breath that meant he was easing into sleep but instead there was a tightness in his body that spread into the air.

"It will be all right," she said. She'd meant to whisper but her voice echoed in the unfurnished room. Lou pulled the blanket up around his neck, exposing half of her naked body to the chilly night air. The other half, pressed against him, felt almost too warm.

THE NEXT MORNING David was patrolling the lawn before Ren had made breakfast.

"I heard somewhere that you have a better chance of seeing deer in the early morning," he said as she came upon him, "when they're feeding."

"Oh, I don't know," Ren said. She thought of commenting that the animals were always eating whenever she or Lou spotted them, but instead she pointed out a woodpecker, high in a hemlock.

Without being asked, David told her he was thinking of quitting his job. For more than ten years he'd been driving a liquor truck and making deliveries to bars and retail liquor stores. A fellow union driver had told him about a need for drivers for a movie to be filmed in Baltimore.

"Packer has worked on two movies already. The money's terrific. If you get on two movies, you end up making more money than working all year for a liquor distributor. Sometimes you drive the actors' trailers. You vacuum the trailers out a little in the morning. Some of the drivers bitch about vacuuming. I don't know. It wouldn't bother me."

Ren and Lou had stayed in a trailer for a couple of nights when Lou's movie was filming in a remote location in Louisiana. The trailer was always spotlessly clean.

When as kids Ren and David had played with his Matchbox trucks and cars, they always divided them up evenly because David was very careful about being fair. He routinely selected the dump truck, fire engine, and crane, allowing Ren the sports car, ambulance, and station wagon to push along the elaborate roadways of Golden Books spread all over the living room and down the hallway to the bathroom. But the trailer attached to a red car was both their favorites. David had timed their use of the trailer — Ren got it for fifteen minutes, he got it for the next fifteen. Ren looked at her brother straight on. His hair was receding and tiny lines branched around his eyes. When Ren and David were young, they had watched the forest behind their little house felled and scraped clean for another row of houses.

"You know," he said, looking off into the trees, "this reminds me of the Valley."

Ren laughed. As a teenager she had gone once to a

party in the Valley. She'd felt totally out of place in the rolling horse country broken up by the estates of privilege.

"Ma said so originally," David said. "Last night. After you and Lou went to bed."

Ren reflected that most of her mother's approval was relayed secondhand. Even though it was diffused that way, she felt warmth spread through her.

"I've been checking this house out," David said, looking toward the roof. "You know, it would really look great if you stained it a deep brown shade. Almost a black."

"We kind of like this weathered look, don't we, Ren?" Lou had appeared behind her. The elements had turned the shingles a silvery gray. She felt his breath against the back of her neck and nodded.

Last night Lou slipped off the blow-up mattress, then whispered to her that his father had died before seeing how his life would work out. Lou had put his arms around Ren, claiming her, pulling her back to the life they had made from their own ambitions and belief in each other, against incredible odds, without precedents. They still needed each other for positive reinforcement against the rest of the world.

Lilly asked what was for breakfast. A light breeze whipped up Ren's mother's peach-colored nightgown as she stepped out of the doorway. The woman's arms were close to her sides, not crossed against her chest in her usual stance of defiance.

"Is that a poor, damn dog laying in the woods out there?" Ren's father asked. They all turned in the direction of his outstretched arm.

"It's a log, for Christ's sake," Ren's mother said, handing him a tissue to wipe his glasses. Ren looked into the shades of brown and beginnings of green, which could camouflage many things.

"It's a log, Dad," David said. He walked toward the

place Ren's father pointed out, and reaching it, kicked the wood for emphasis. "See?" he called.

ON SUNDAY AFTERNOON while they were exchanging good-byes, Ren's mother produced a small package and quickly handed it to Ren as if it were of no more significance than a litter bag she needed to dispose of. "I guess you two are big wheels now. I guess you don't need your old mother's advice."

Ren immediately reached inside the bag and pulled out a small, framed sampler, cross-stitched in purple threads, inside a green and pink border of flowers. "Wherever you wander, wherever you roam, be happy and healthy, and glad to come home."

The car door made a cranking noise, then slammed shut. David turned the ignition and called out the window, "Maybe next time we'll see the deer."

Ren's father, sitting in the backseat next to Lilly, looked smaller than when he'd arrived. Ren watched the car wobble off down the driveway. She wondered if her mother and father and brother understood that her house wasn't a temporary stopover, some phase, as her mother called so many of Ren's convictions, but their home. And while she and Lou would never live in Baltimore or Staten Island again, she regretted her pride, wished she could have eased their minds by telling them that there *were* family cords, thick as exhaust hoses. And there *were* deer. She'd take pictures.

"Ren," Lou said, as she heard the car backfiring in the distance. "I couldn't have stood another day of it, I'm sorry. 'Why don't you do this?' 'Why not move the couch over there?' 'I don't want to interfere, but. . . .' How many times did you hear that one?" Lou paused. "Who do they think they are?"

She softly answered his question. "My family."

"I'm your family now," Lou said. He paused. "Why go out of your way for them? They never believed in us. Nobody even asked about your acting or my writing all weekend." He sighed. "They didn't even think we'd stay married."

Ren thought, nobody but your family could make you go mute in front of injustice. Nobody but your family could threaten your most essential relationship.

"You could have seen them off," Ren said.

He ignored her reprimand. "What the hell are we going to do with that?" He pointed to the giant smirking cat holding the birdbath, which not one bird had approached since it had been positioned on the lawn.

"They thought it looked cute," she said.

"They want to make our place look like their white trash house. And then what happens when my mother gets in the act? It'll look like goddamn Coney Island up here."

Lou's eyes were wild, frightened. Ren recognized the look he had when actors were changing his lines, forgetting his intentions, disregarding all his weeks of writing and rewriting.

"They're just afraid, I don't know, that they're losing us," she said.

"That's a laugh. They just want us on their own terms." He took the cross-stitching from her and threw it against the huge oak in front of the house. When she heard the glass frame shatter, she thought for a moment that she'd screamed.

THE SUN WAS JUST starting to set when Lou came to her. She put her arms around him more easily than she'd anticipated and for an instant every thought went out of her head. He felt almost fragile after her mother. She smelled his aftershave, rubbed against his smooth face. He sighed into her hair and she found herself getting weak behind the knees as if she'd had two or three drinks. Then she sensed hunger, a rumbling in her stomach that she'd ignored for hours.

As she looked up out the windows of the sunroom, she saw the deer, three feet from the glass, its dusky coat almost invisible, its head and neck lowered to the ground to eat. Beyond it, as if she'd just put on her glasses, she saw two, five, a whole herd emerge from the dull background. It almost seemed to her that they'd been there all along. Her arms tightened around Lou. The first deer she'd noticed instantly raised its head, tail flicked. She breathed shallowly, carefully. At her slightest movement, they would bolt away.

II

Around Them

6
Opening

Five months ago I paid off the last of the creditors, Tommy Whippermann, from a financial services firm called Wachovia. Which had come to sound more and more like "watch over ya". Five hours from now I'll be shaking hands with De Niro. Probably talking about something like heart. I hear "Bobby" saying, "Lou, this film of yours really has heart."

Even though old Tommy's never seen me face-to-face, I have no trouble believing he could pick me out of a lineup. He's been with me all along. As soon as I quit sneaking around to avoid his calls, stopped monitoring his messages on my answering machine and let him know what was what, he was actually more concerned about my career than my damn family. I sent him a couple of bucks every now and then. Interest on purchases that had long since worn out. He asked me how the script was coming. Even gave me a fairly good note once — "You probably could use a little more action right from the get-go."

The way all this happened sounds like a story. One everyone's heard before. But I swear it's true. I wrote a play. Actually, I wrote many plays, but this one received a fair amount of media attention.

The evening *Past Tense* closed, the play that really started this big ball rolling in the Hollywood direction, Ren and I left the cast party more than a little drunk. We were walking and I grabbed her. Kissed her right there in the middle of Seventh Avenue. Then the light changed and we opened our eyes to an onslaught of light and honking as oncoming traffic swerved to either side of us. And we just held there because what else could we do?

A Hollywood producer called me (in the print interview he says he grabbed onto me backstage). "Lou," he said. "I love it. I wish I could make a movie of *Past Tense*." Although the play had generally gotten mixed reviews, I thought it was the best thing I'd written.

"Really?" I'm a ten-year-old being offered a submachine gun.

"But I don't see that happening." He mentioned casting, and instantly I knew he was referring to the sexual issue — black man and white woman.

"Uh huh," I said. The submachine gun shrinks to a popgun.

"Do you have any screenplays?"

"Screenplays? Sure, I have a screenplay."

"Send it to me, Lou. I'll see what I can do." He paused. "A screenplay with different kinds of characters. If you know what I mean," he said.

As soon as I hung up I ran a hot tub of water. Got in with my wife. We have our most important discussions in the tub. Renata eased in on one side of the spigot. I spread against the other end, shoulders relaxed along the lip of the porcelain. Then, after a few minutes of giving in to the heat, we sank deeper under the water and kind of molded into each other.

Ren said, "Why don't you turn one of your stage plays into a screenplay?" Like my grandmother, Ren believes that most things are meant for more than one use, and people who don't figure this out are basically lazy. Recycling is right up Ren's alley.

So I took *Blue Corners,* a play that had received no more than an upstate reading, checked out a few books on screenwriting from the library, and sat down with my portable typewriter.

"Where's the screenplay?" the producer called to ask.

"I'm having a problem with my computer," I said, sure he was strolling the gardens of his Brentwood estate with his cell phone. Cut to me sandwiched between the pull-out sofa and my desk, a scarred door spread across two file cabinets. Open books, papers, empty coffee mugs line the arm of the sofa and every surface of the "desk". There was less room than if I'd been typing in the bathtub.

The producer told me to buy a new computer. I laughed. All I wanted to buy was time.

On his second call, I told him I thought the problem was my printer. I slept four hours at a clip the next few days. Writing late into the night. Thinking screenplay the whole time I worked my bi-weekly stint cleaning a Unitarian church. I became so distracted at the other part-time job — developing reams of vacation photos — that my boss thought I was getting sick. I verified his concern by calling in two days in a row. I did feel sick. Feverish and driven, focused on one project mentally, everything else around me a mass of irrelevant detail. I finally mailed the screenplay.

The producer and his partner made a conference call. Asked who I envisioned playing the lead.

"Oh, I don't know. Hoffman, De Niro, Hackman." I was still giddy with accomplishment and lack of sleep.

"Good, good," they said in unison. Then one of them said, "I'll give Bobby a call."

Bobby.

I met Bobby during the shooting in Louisiana. Had a talk with him before we started filming. Even drinks a couple of times. But tonight's the opening. It's official. People tell me you can live with somebody five, ten years, but when you marry them you still go weak in the knees.

Even though everything seems to have fallen into place, I can't quite see my name (spelled correctly) in the opening credits. Ren said we could be confident the movie would be made when I got the check with more zeros than should fit on a pale-blue piece of paper. When Ren delivered it to our accountant, he joked that the two of them should run off together. She said after that the check didn't feel like money. More like a ticket to Belize.

I've tried to believe this would happen. That eventually I'd see my own film on a regulation-size movie screen. Not just our television with its screen no bigger than a piece of typing paper held sideways. But somehow, deep in the recesses of my gut, marked by an Irish grandmother and years of theater's false promises, I've had this sense that something would go wrong. "Gee, Lou, I'm sorry about all this. And, by the way, I'll be needing that pale-blue check back."

Ren's off scouting up a bottle of champagne and I'm laying out my garb in our friend Rick's apartment to make myself believe. The shirt, the tux, the cummerbund, the socks. The socks. The socks. Shoes? Fuck. My shoes —my favorite boots — are standing at the front door back home in Connecticut.

My good-luck boots. I bump into Ren on my way out to a shoe store. Practically knocking the expensive champagne she's cradling out of her arms.

Whenever I'm looking for a quick cup of coffee, like on my way to a rehearsal, I pass a shoe store every ten feet. Today, groceries and delis pop up so frequently Madison Avenue resembles a mall's food concession. When I ask two different pedestrians if they know where a shoe store is, I get looks meant for someone who's brandishing a knife, announcing he's going to cut the tongues out of every pair of shoes on the East Side.

Manhattan is frustrating in this unique way: Whatever you need or want at any particular time can't be more than a few blocks away. And yet, it's always in the opposite direction. In Milwaukee, this is not a problem.

I hop the subway over to Macy's. Settle on the standard black, over-priced issue. With that blood-colored bag in my hand I feel invincible. "Writer in Search of Shoes Murdered in Subway on Night of Film Opening" just isn't pithy enough.

I get back and Ren's crying. She doesn't cry often, but when she does it's big time. She's crying and pointing at her neck and I find myself instinctively grabbing for my heart.

She wrenches my hand away from my chest. Pulls both my arms around her. Mumbles into my face, "Hives." Then proceeds to rip open her blouse with such drama a button whizzes past my eye and hits the wall. There all across her chest, up and down the length of her neck, are enough little welts to advertise a mosquito convention. Beyond her, hanging in the doorway to the bedroom, is Ren's attire for tonight — a deep-blue *strapless* dress.

"God," she says, "I haven't had anything like this since I was a kid and got all anxious before the Iowa tests. Remember the Iowa tests?"

She begins to cry harder. While I'm patting her back trying to calm her, I can smell the pages of those standardized tests. The pressure to pick the correct title for a paragraph you'd just read. What would be the capper for tonight's adventure — "Dressing Up" or "New York Catastrophes"?

"How about 'Opening Night'?" Ren says.

I grab the champagne. "I can't believe with all your performances this hasn't happened until now."

She resists cold towel compresses but finally gives in

after I refill her champagne glass. Does Ren's body sense a problem that I don't? Will tonight be a disaster instead of a turning point?

"Maybe I'll start getting ready," I say. I'm pacing around the leather sofa on which Ren is reclining in mottled splendor.

"We've got almost two hours before we have to leave. You'll get wrinkled."

"I'll take wrinkled over frenzied any day." I run the shower. Ren drains the last of the champagne. Gets in with me.

"Don't you think you should stay under the icy towels a little longer?"

"I thought I'd try some heat," she says and lathers up my back. Champagne's the best mood enhancer in the world.

My first grant eight years ago — that three-thousand dollar affirmation of my talent — sent Ren on an out-of-character trip to the liquor store with all our weekly food money. She spent our budget on a bottle of Moët and the next six days we ate raisin bran.

Ren's calming down and, in response, the bumps on her neck do seem to have dissolved. But she says it's an illusion. Her body has merely reddened all over in the hot water.

My clothes spread across the bed and hang from the doorknobs. A body blown apart into its singular pieces. I slide and slip articles of clothing onto my arms and legs. I've got the preparation perfectly paced — clothes, hair, a little wine, more time with the hair, a couple of photographs, a piece of gum and we're out the door. But as soon as I'm in my shirt and feel it all slack around my wrists, I know there will be no wine time, no pictures.

"Ren, this shirt takes cufflinks."

"Maybe Rick's got some you can borrow," she says

nonchalantly. I hear her poking around on the top of his dresser.

"Terry doesn't even own a tie," I say heading for the door, the unfastened cuffs flopping at my wrists. This time I don't screw around asking strangers to make subcontextual references about clothing. I grab a cab and head back across town to Macy's. All the while the cab driver is running red lights, honking and swearing, I'm thinking, "The single most important day of my career and I'm not going to make it."

Macy's is a freak show. I race to find the correct counter for cufflinks praying I won't run into the guy who sold me shoes an hour-and-a-half ago. When I complain to the clerk about the price of the boring lumps of metal, he sighs, rummages under the counter and presents me with two regulation safety pins. Maybe. Maybe. And then I spot them. "What about those?" He holds up two tiny skulls. $9.95. "Perfect," I say. I swear he slid them out of his own pocket.

I arrive at the apartment just in time for Ren to set the camera timer and run into the picture with me. She's wearing a black shawl around her neck to cover the hives. I'm disheveled, sweaty. The cufflinks guy might as well have plugged me into a cannon and fired me uptown.

Now we can't find a cab. All dressed up, Ren and I keep running for cabs that strangers, a half a block south, snatch away from us. We finally catch one on a side street and head cross town.

Peter Max's studio is full of art and lights. Sequined outfits vibrate by. "Fabulous." "Great." "Terrific." The mixture of alcohol and too much smiling makes me light-headed. Ten minutes into it and I'm sweating like I'm in a sauna. Ren's hot, too, but she's keeping the big black shawl in place.

Anyone who comes by and claps me on the back must

be able to detect how damp I am. But they don't say much. They're holding back until the film is shown and there's consensus on its merits. Or lack thereof.

I dab at my forehead with the purple cocktail napkin until Ren says, "My God, Lou." She swipes at my skin with a couple of tissues she pulls from her tiny purse. "You look like some grocer's been trying to stamp you with prices."

Before we moved to Connecticut, we lived for a while in my sister's basement in Meadow, New York. On the creek behind the house was an old Finnish sauna the size of an outhouse. Ren and I used to cook up the stove to nearly two hundred degrees, sweat every impurity and worry out of our systems, then leap into the icy fast-moving water. I wish Peter Max had a creek so I could flush some of the bullshit out of my body.

The afternoon I got the call that the movie was a go, the sky was brilliant blue, the sun huge and untouched by clouds. As soon as Ren showed up from work I took her down to the sauna. Picked her up and threw her into the creek. All her clothes on. She screamed and came after me. And we doused ourselves of the life we'd led until that point.

"Howdy," Clem says, surprising me. Clem weighs about three hundred, which makes him stand out in this crowd of people who have opportunity wrapped so tightly around them they're thin as crudités. Who'd believe that Porter, the character I created, would be played by an actor I could actually have a drink with.

But even Clem's not mentioning the film. Everyone is superstitious. As if one wrong comment could conjure up failure. Or success. The only discussion comes from the *Entertainment Tonight* interviewer and he's got Bobby pinned behind the drink table.

"There's the man," Clem says and heads off toward De Niro.

"Clem's a pretty nice guy," Ren says.

"Sure," I say. "But I think I like Porter better."

"Oh, why don't you relax?" she says, sliding the shawl off her upper body. The pattern of tiny welts has almost disappeared.

THREE BLOCKS AWAY, the movie is running — music, action, dialogue. A couple of scenes have been cut since the last time I saw *Cornered,* the Hollywood title for *Blue Corners,* at a private screening. But my name's still intact and when it pops up on the screen Ren squeezes my hand.

Somehow I can't let go and follow the narrative. I'm remembering the different musky towns where filming took place, and even farther back when a guy everyone called Bayou Boy drove us around and pointed out location possibilities. I'm remembering the movie when I felt closest to it. When it was still part of everyone's imagination.

Even as applause fills the theater, I expect to hear one voice rise above the clatter of approval, a "force" to stand out screaming, "No. Stop. What are they doing? Do they know what they're doing?" And that interruption will signal the end of my involvement in film. But the clapping goes on.

On the way out, I sense Ren hanging back in the lobby listening attentively for comments, reactions. I swear I hear somebody sigh so deeply it sounds like a wave has knocked the breath from his body. And I'm thinking ahead to the next step. I'm thinking, "Oh, no. The critics. I'm a dead man."

It's a cool, yet clear, night almost the color of Ren's dress. As we're meandering the couple of blocks to the restaurant I'm feeling lighter and lighter. Falling off me into the sounds of traffic are all the years of comments like "have-you-got-a-real-job-yet-or-not?" and even Tommy Whippermann, every goddamn week, chipper as ever, "So how's the screenplay coming?"

Then, very clearly, right in front of me, one photographer calls to another, "Anybody else here? Anybody else worth stickin' around for?"

I want to yell, how about the writer, Bozo?

On the way into the restaurant, we're flanked by De Niro and, on the other side, a guy who matches my mental image of Tommy Whippermann. Short, glasses sliding to the middle of his nose, large hands with fingers the size of Vienna sausages. I try to say something to De Niro but the crowd has taken him over. And for an instant I'm overcome with this weird feeling that Tommy's trailing me, about to say, "There's a bit of a problem we need to take care of." But soon the memories of not being able to make it into Manhattan to see one of my plays — because I didn't have train fare — are falling off like so many crumbs from the flaky dinner rolls.

After coffee, somebody hands us presents. Rolled up posters and boxes of chocolates that we open in the cab and stare at. They're the size of chocolate-chip cookies. And they're not all show either, they're delicious. Ren gives the cab driver one.

Ren says it's chilly, but I'm not feeling it. The city's a surreal blur of color and motion. Ren's settled in the crook of my arm. The movie's actually on the screen. And De Niro's words which I've woven into a compliment — "The movie's got guts" — play back in my mind. I have it all.

At the apartment, Ren feeds me another mammoth chocolate. We walk into the living room that's dark. New York dark — there's always a hint of light slipping in from somewhere. The next thing I know we're on the floor and our best clothes are flung in different directions. The new skull cufflinks ping across the floor, and not too far off somebody's stereo system sends Al Green's "Tired of Being Alone" slinking up the shaft way.

7
One-Way Street

When the main road near our house in Connecticut turned one-way, people on our side street started going to bed early. Houses competed to be the first to darken on those black-green, late summer evenings as strangers, disoriented by the state's new directional signs, pulled off that road and onto our residential one, then pounded on the door at the nearest beacon of light.

Ours was six in, so initially we had buffers against the lost and frantic drivers. The first couple of weeks, I was sympathetic to the confusion of those who often drove more than five miles in the wrong direction before ending up at the Country Deli, which closed precisely at eight. But when our neighbors started faking bedtime, and people I didn't know broke into my evenings with challenges like, "How in the hell do I get back on the highway?" I lost patience. By the third interruption, I had taken on the gait of a Frankenstein when I opened the door. I was sure I'd seen a flicker of candlelight deep in my neighbor's house, and when Lou said to forget it, I told him he could get the door next time.

A week before Lou's fortieth birthday, the interstate was still not adequately marked with signs indicating exits north and south. I provided detailed directions for everyone we'd invited to the party, in addition to noting our new, unlisted phone number.

Between the time *Cornered* was released nationwide and Lou's new play, *Daily Life,* began auditioning Off-Broadway, the phone had rung endlessly with the voices of strangers or acquaintances from the distant past. Lengthy messages filled the answering tape with longing. Lou anguished over whether becoming unlisted in Connecticut would make him appear too aloof. After he got a call from deep in the Midwest, I pushed him to chance it.

"I don't know what the guy wanted from me," Lou said, genuinely confused. "He said we went to high school together. Said I'd probably remember him as Junior. I don't remember any Junior." Lou looked up at me. "I think he wanted me to read a science fiction book he wrote."

Lou's birthday party had me looking forward to an evening without strangers — tireless salesmen, hungry actors, old girlfriends, and lost motorists. And though I hadn't planned it, the celebration with friends would be twofold. Any trepidation Lou might feel about his age would be deflected by the favorable review *Daily Life* had just received in *The New York Times*.

Carl and Beth arrived before Lou was out of the shower. I'd known Carl as long as Lou, but Beth only about a year and a half. All of Carl's girlfriends were small and dark. Two of them even had the same first name.

Before I said a word, Carl held his hands open in a gesture of surrender. "We didn't bring anything," he said as his enlarged Adam's apple bobbed against his throat. "Didn't think you'd need anything."

I was surprised, but quickly asked them about work (they taught at two different community colleges) and they groaned simultaneously. By the time Lou made his way downstairs, Amy and Kent had also shown up.

"Great house you have here," Kent said, looking at the beamed ceiling, then slipping his hands into his pockets.

"It's the same house we had six months ago when you stopped by," Lou said.

"It's still nice," Amy said softly and slid her arm protectively through her husband's.

I watched Lou deciding whether to ask Kent about business, and then he asked. Back when Lou was still daydreaming about seeing one of his plays performed, he had worked for Amy and Kent's carpet-cleaning service. Though Kent said Lou deserved success, I knew he considered it good luck, not unlike winning the lottery. He had never witnessed Lou drag his tired body out of bed at five in the morning to finish a scene before trudging off to clean somebody's ivory-colored wall-to-wall Axminster. Today Kent was hesitant, holding himself back as if Lou were only pretending they'd once had something in common.

"How's Eric?" I asked of their four-year-old.

"It's hard to keep up with him," Kent said proudly.

"Where's Jake?" Lou wanted to know.

"I can't believe he's not here," Carl said. Jake was the first at any gathering, especially if food was a feature. Jake once confessed to devouring so much at an all-you-can-eat fireman's breakfast, he'd had to lie down under one of the picnic tables. Then he went around the back of the firehouse, threw up, and a few minutes later got himself a fresh plate of pancakes, fried eggs and sausage links.

I was never sure that, if asked, Jake wouldn't move right in with Lou and me, even though he had his own wife and a son out on Long Island. He made me claustrophobic the way he pushed into our plans as if wanting Lou's life instead of his own and, in one instance I'd never shared with Lou, of wanting me as well.

Lou and Jake had gone to high school together, Jake the privileged heir of attorneys and Lou the kid who'd had to tunnel his way past a family of laborers to reach turf of his own. Jake had romantic and inaccurate ideas about the working class. He was a newspaper court reporter but after work when he wrote fiction he made a conscious effort to create characters who smoked cigars, gambled and fraternized with countless women. I wondered if Jake knew that when Lou informed his father that he was going to study writing, Lou Senior had replied, "It's about time. I never have been able to make out a damn thing you write."

"This has got to be Jake," Lou said, going for the door, but it was Vivien Farrow, our neighbor on the far side, the one dazed motorists questioned if Lou and I were out or asleep. Vivien wore a black lacy coverup over what looked like a bra top and a pair of shorts.

Even as Lou greeted Vivien appreciatively, I knew he was disappointed not to see Jake standing there. He was relying on Jake to praise the review *Daily Life* had received. No one else had congratulated him, not even his agent. Most people assumed Lou had only written plays as a venue to the big screen; they didn't understand that, to him, plays were now more important than ever. Maybe it was all simpler than envy. Maybe people just thought Lou had had his share of success, regardless of format.

Vivien wouldn't have read the *Times*. She had grown up in Connecticut and scanned only the local paper. Her husband owned two local liquor stores and advertised his services as an "all-round handy man". He charged seventy-five dollars to drive people to the New York airports.

Noticing that Lou looked behind her and out the door, Vivien asked, "Did someone get lost?"

The next guest to arrive was Michael and Lou asked, "Where's Diana?"

Michael said, "Wouldn't come. She thinks you've sold out."

"What?" Lou asked, almost shutting the door in the face of his sister and brother-in-law, Angela and Terry.

"Relax," Michael said. "It doesn't matter what she thinks. We're separated."

Now I was the one to say, "What?" Then, "When did this happen?"

Michael said, "Just about the time I said I was coming to your party."

"This is some spread you've got here, brother," Lou's sister Angela said as she strode across the hardwood floors.

Showing the couple through the house, Lou muttered, "How can anybody say I've sold out? I'm doing exactly what I've done for the past fifteen years. Only now I'm getting paid for it."

Then he asked — a little too loudly — if Angela had seen the review of his play. But no one else in hearing range — Carl or Beth or Amy — picked up on the question.

"It was great," Angela said, explaining that their older sister had read it to her over the phone. "Just don't get too big for us," she said, as if a family were a standard-ized size, one that couldn't grow.

"You still do plays?" Terry asked. Lou only nodded. Terry had lost the small finger on his right hand. He was a heavy machinery mechanic, but the accident had oc-curred during a bar fight.

"Why write plays when they don't make any money?" Terry asked. Blunt and confrontational in every aspect of his life, Terry was often described as someone who didn't "pull any punches". Lou had never particularly liked him.

Hollywood was the ultimate goal. Everyone said so, not just Terry. In reality, Lou and I knew that Hollywood was where you severed yourself from your creation as soon as your pen scratched the back of the check. With plays you had some degree of control over what you wrote, Lou had repeated to me just that morning.

"Where's Jake?" Angela asked.

"It's not like him," Lou said. "He's always the first." Once I considered that maybe Jake and Lou had been brothers in some other life, Lou was so blind to Jake's faults — a selfish man who liked, no needed, to turn every social situation to himself.

When Lou's older sister, Beth, arrived we served dinner. "I wonder what happened," Lou whispered, and I knew he was referring again to Jake.

In the kitchen I reached behind Lou to replenish a platter of raw vegetables. "Lou, even if he shows up he may not mention the review," I said gently.

"He will. I know he saw it."

Lou walked to the sink to fill a glass pitcher with water, then went back to the company before I could further discredit his friend.

As Lou was opening birthday gifts that I'd told everyone not to bring, I couldn't help but look around at the roomful of friends, imagining, perhaps unfairly, their envy, their waiting for Lou to fail. Consolation is probably easier than compliments for most people, I thought. Yet these weren't most people; these were friends we'd known for years.

But what if our friends' reactions were portentous? Their collective reservations at our moving from a dingy apartment to a house in the country, changing our drink-of-choice from Genesee Cream Ale to champagne and buying coats from Eddie Bauer instead of Bradlees seemed so negative that it could damage my ambition and Lou's.

Lou was opening a huge form covered in white paper. "It's a rocking chair," Angela was exclaiming. Terry explained that he'd wanted to give Lou an engraved pistol instead.

"I could use a pistol about now," I said, but even Lou didn't hear me. I had no idea why the support of everyone in the room suddenly had me on edge.

Lou next opened a box containing an electric massager. He said, "This seems like a Jake gift," and looked around the room as if truly expecting to see his friend camouflaged in the curtains.

"It's from me," Michael called. "You can use it on all the Hollywood babes."

"I'll use it on you, you joker," Lou said.

Later in the kitchen Lou poured a few brandies and said, "Nobody but my sister has mentioned the review." He looked tense and defiant. He was past the hurt and now angry that Jake hadn't appeared. If I weren't his wife, I wondered if I too might have withheld praise if it pointed up my own unfulfilled ambitions.

"A good review is a test of friendship," I said and kissed him on the forehead, then headed back to the guests, all those people convincing themselves that success had changed *him*.

Suddenly it sounded as if a twenty-pound bag of potatoes had been thrown against the front door. I walked through the living room expecting another stranger, a drunk, a dangerous intruder interrupted in the middle of some well-thought-out crime.

It was Jake. His face was red, the vein on the side of his neck stood out like a garden snake and, in the cooling dark air outside the front door, he was sweating.

He spoke in loud, staccato accusations. "I couldn't get to your house. The road's all screwed up. Your phone number is different."

"I put it all down in the letter, Jake. I spelled everything out," I said.

"I guess I didn't read that part." In the porch light his hair looked gray.

"I got here by driving down the wrong side of a one-way and then somebody ran me off the road."

Jake and Lou went outside with flashlights to evaluate the damage to Jake's front bumper and headlight. By the time they came back inside, Jake's intensity had turned on Lou. "Congratulations, you bastard." He took a breath. "I don't mean the birthday. We all have birthdays. I mean the whole deal." He lowered his voice. "You're killin' 'em, pal."

A couple of people clapped Lou on the back then. But shortly after, the party started breaking up. I could hear Jake telling the departing guests about his young son's aikido lessons and his brother's band.

"It's driving me crazy," Jake said. I was almost disappointed to realize that Jake was referring to his wife.

Eventually Lou and Jake listened to Motown. Then they drank beer and sang "Ferry Cross the Mersey" in decent harmony as I began to clean up from the party. But after loading the dishwasher, I had a beer with them before heading upstairs.

"Do you remember anybody named Junior?" Lou asked.

"Junior?" Jake said.

Each step creaked with the comments of old friends and strangers. By the time I reached the top, Lou and Jake had started in on "Time Won't Let Me." Their voices, loud and resonant, completely covered any sounds of traffic.

8
The Willing

At Renata's 20th high school reunion, a gynecologist, a gym teacher, a speech therapist, a legal secretary, a lawyer, a singer, two nurses, and a born-again Christian absorbed by the social life of her church showed up. Another lived on her settlement from a sexual harassment suit and someone else managed a nursing facility for the elderly. The senior class president had become a migrant laborer, whom no one had been successful in contacting. And Renata, at thirty-eight, actor-in-waiting.

Frederick Willing, the name of the founder and the school, had always sounded to Renata like a command — a place you were supposed to be, a way you were obliged to act, a symbol of how you were meant to think. Frederick Willing was long dead and even the school no longer existed. Over the course of Renata's seven years there, girls' schools had gone out of fashion. By the time she graduated, only seventeen young women comprised her class.

They came without their men. Spouses and lovers would erect a barricade, they said, which could not be completely penetrated in the approximately eight hours they would all spend together in the suite of The Calvert, a Baltimore luxury hotel. Renata had to agree that no matter how extensively she'd described her boarding school to her husband, certain things just couldn't be communicated to an outsider — no matter how long you'd been married.

There was little talk of the men initially. But photographs of houses and children soon began to appear in the middle of conversations. And every once in a while in one of the glossy squares that hesitated momentarily in Renata's fingers, she glimpsed a male, often in the background, or out-of-focus, or cropped off just above the nose.

"I don't have a picture of Fred but I've got his Corvette," Shirley called from near the window. Then she pointed down at a white convertible. Renata found it hard to visualize Shirley, in her perfectly tailored beige linen suit and stiffly-coiffed blonde curls, whipping against the wind. Shirley was a head nurse at Union Memorial in Baltimore and she'd planned the reunion.

"They go through this mid-life thing and all they think about is sports cars," Chris said. Chris had put on thirty pounds since graduation. The weight hadn't made her more self-conscious but seemed to buffer her from awkwardness.

"It's good that's all yours thinks about," Gina said and looked away from the window. Gina was also a nurse but at a different hospital from Shirley's.

"Leslie wanted to bring a date today," Shirley said, changing the subject. She raised her eyes at the word "date". "I told her she couldn't."

Some of the women briefly mentioned their careers and families but once the packets of photos had circled the group and were tucked back into purses and pockets, "remember" preceded nearly every sentence. Each girl at The Willing had been assigned a daily chore, which changed four times during the school year. The list of jobs, all intended to "build character", had included dry mopping and wet mopping, dish washing, dusting, polishing, weeding, wiping, raking leaves and shoveling snow. Renata recalled precisely the first job she'd had twenty-seven years earlier. The sour odor of the stiff gray mop she'd dipped into a metal pail filled with warm water had never left her. She'd pushed the desks into neat rows and swiped at the red floor pocked by the small round feet of the desks and dreamed the indentations had come from high heels. She'd fantasized herself grown-up and dancing all night, making marks that would never wash away.

Because some of them had attended the boarding institution since elementary school, they'd witnessed their uniforms lose uniformity — breasts and hips taking shape against the wine-colored jumpers and white blouses. They'd watched one another at mixers when a bus load of boys would be imported like so many food supplies. Some of the girls had slipped off to the parking lot between dances; some clung to the opposite sex during slow dances until one of many chaperons pried them apart; and a few, frozen with curiosity like Renata, hung on the sidelines to study the amazing transformations.

The day following a dance was always full of talk — which boy was the cutest, who had gone the farthest, who had danced the closest without getting caught. They gossiped almost that same way now, as if their lives since graduation had been one long dance, as if they hadn't married and accepted the lives of guys who'd once been the object of their competition.

"Help yourself," Holly said, opening Tupperware containers and setting out plates of hors d'oeuvres — tiny sandwiches cut into hearts and triangles, flaky pastries, vegetables and fruits sliced in exotic ways and miniature portions of meats and fish each set against a doily. It reminded Renata of another crowded room and abundance of food — her parents' dining room after her uncle's funeral.

"I thought we were eating in the hotel dining room," Shirley said, frowning over the plates of food.

Holly ignored Shirley and turned to Renata. "Oh, this was easy to do, Lizzy Frizzy," Holly said. The nickname referred to Renata's curly hair, which she'd spent three years at The Willing trying to contain. She had ironed it, combed it with gels, pressed it onto rollers constructed from frozen orange juice containers. Lou, the first person who genuinely liked the natural state of her hair, encouraged her to let it go. Now it stood loose and defiant about her face, a protective frame. The veil of security was welcome. All the other women, even her once best friend Ellen, now a gynecologist married to a surgeon, wore good jewelry and a stylish outfit, and appeared settled into financial security. Renata sensed a twinge of her old exclusion — the scholarship girl admitted to the coterie of privilege solely on the strength of her intelligence and her mother's brash persistence.

Renata was dressed in leggings and a tunic-length pastel jacket, and with her wild hair she hoped she reflected all the changes in her since she'd been at The Willing. She had no photos of children or dogs. When asked, she spoke frankly of her commercials or voice-overs for Taster's Choice, Tide and Crest. She didn't bring up the hundreds of roles she'd lost, the hours of anticipation followed by bitter rejection.

"I knew one of us would get on TV," Holly said, and squeezed Renata's forearm.

Renata mentioned *Cornered*. She used her husband's accomplishment when she felt her own didn't sustain conversation.

"Hey. I *think* I saw that," Carly said. Carly was petite, her features sharp and hair dyed black. Renata wanted to reply that she was glad the movie had been so memorable but instead mentioned De Niro to prod Carly's memory.

"Talk about celebrities," Holly said and reached for her large white purse. "I can't believe I forgot to show you all this."

"I think Holly's standing beside one of those cutouts of Oliver North," Chris teased as she studied the five-by-seven signed photo.

"No sir," Holly said, "It's the real thing."

Holly had been the first person Renata had spotted in the lobby of the hotel, its every surface polished to a high shine. Holly stood out, too, with a huge pink bow in her shoulder-length hair and a dress of multi-colored flowers the size of baseballs. Swatches of lace clung to the cuffs and bodice of the dress. The first girl her age Renata knew who had sex, Holly revealed that she had no idea what was happening when the high school senior had taken her to the dark backseat of his car. And a couple of months later when he left with no explanation, Holly cried at any mention of sexual intimacy and couldn't be comforted.

Now Holly served on Christian Light Fellowship church committees, which stressed parental intervention in every aspect of a minor's life from textbook selection to television advertising. She was the mother of a seventeen-year-old retarded daughter and the wife of a man who, she proudly proclaimed, had his own bedroom.

After the young and handsome room-service guy knocked on the door and asked if the group needed anything, he said, "Enjoy your afternoon, ladies."

"Wow, was he checking you out," Holly said to Renata.

"Holly," Renata said, "he was about nineteen." Holly shrugged her shoulders but Renata wondered if Holly was imagining show business affairs and clandestine meetings with fellow actors.

Although Renata knew she was being judgmental about these women, the connection of long ago, before relationships with the opposite sex grew so complicated, remained. But as they discussed those women who weren't among them — the Latin teacher with a fixation on crocodiles, the class secretary who'd become a model and was later ensnared by drugs — Renata saw that back then their lives were more problematic than she'd recognized. Old images flashed through her mind. Spinster teachers who drank; young women, now designated anorexics and bulimics, whom Renata had known as girls who were getting smaller and thinner; and others, those who insisted on not regressing, boldly sneaking cigarettes and sips of wine from stashes deep in their gray lockers.

Renata remembered asking the withered woman at the head of her dining room table if she could scrape her plate of the remnants of creamed chipped beef on toast or shepherd's pie or chicken chow mein, and be excused to run the length of the field-hockey green. She'd walk the long hallways, shaded the dark shiny brown-black of beetles, to the outside. Maneuvering a ball all to herself, she tapped and tapped it down the grassy straightaway in the direction of a far-off goal. Along one side of the hockey field, pink and white dogwood trees seemed to bloom for months in contrast to the cold gray stone of the school, though now Renata was sure they had only lasted a couple of weeks at best.

Someone urged Meryl to sing the school song. Meryl cleared her throat nervously and said she couldn't sing any more.

"Come on, Meryl," Shirley said. "You know I sound like a cat under a garbage lid."

In school, Meryl had an other-worldly voice that Renata even then had recognized as destiny. The voice wasn't light and ephemeral and girlish, but clear and full, resonant with determination. When Meryl sang, every note assured, Renata felt ambivalence, confusion, all silly concerns pushed aside. Meryl had been the only one among them guaranteed success. Whatever she achieved, Renata knew *she'd* have to work very hard at; Meryl had natural talent.

Meryl touched her throat and said, "I can't sustain my voice for more than three minutes any more. No one really knows why it happened. Basically my vocal chords don't work in synch."

In the silence that followed, Meryl bent forward and reached deep into a canvas bag on the floor. She produced a thick stack of photographs, then identified the operas and characters she'd played and the cities where she'd performed.

"I didn't know if I'd be able to do this," she said softly. "You know, look at all these again."

"Isn't there a procedure you can have done?" Carly asked.

As Renata watched Meryl's photographs making the rounds, it seemed to her that the larger picture, the one of their lives, had shattered and everyone held a piece that didn't quite fit.

"What are you going to do?" Carly asked softly. So many sleepless nights Renata had asked herself the same question. What will I do if I can't make it as an actor?

"Well, for one thing, I'm getting married," Meryl said and brightened. "Ian and I are getting married in six weeks." She produced another picture, this one from her wallet.

Ian looked fifteen years younger than anyone in the room. As Renata studied his portrait, Meryl explained that years ago she'd divorced a man who couldn't live with her artistic ambitions. "So at least one part of my life is working out," Meryl said.

"No small accomplishment," Gina said.

Renata sighed more loudly than she'd meant to. In

her own way, she was as handicapped as Meryl. She'd never gotten her "real break"; no reviewer had praised her enough to send her beyond adequacy and into the realm of brilliance. How long did you wait for the break before you gave up and settled for simpler pleasures? Would she, like Meryl, decide subconsciously that she couldn't handle real success? Lou reminded Renata as he did himself, "You can sabotage your future if you're afraid."

"Maybe we'll have a baby," Meryl said.

"And Ellen can deliver it," Renata blurted out. She had an intense urge to squeeze everyone in the room into a wedge that would secure the door against the injustices just beyond.

Ellen said softly, "I'd love to have another baby." The candor of the remark surprised Renata. For years Ellen had been her best friend but today, dressed in a suit and thick gold necklace, Ellen looked impenetrable. With three children from his first marriage, her husband had urged Ellen to remain childless. After four years together, she had finally persuaded him to agree to one child of their own, but, in return, she'd consented to return to her practice six weeks after the baby was born.

"Does anybody think going to a girls' school wrecked her social life?" Carly interrupted. She was one of three single women in the room and the only one who had never married. She described once going out with a man so heavily sedated that he drooled during dinner.

"I don't think so," Chris said. Chris had married Brian, the football player she'd dated her last two years at The Willing. "I mean you didn't go to an all girls' college, did you?"

Carly shook her head and tried to pursue her thought, but Renata said, "I did. My college let women know right off that they were capable, expected even, of doing anything men did. We ran our own show." She paused. "Nobody lost an election for class president because of her sex."

"But maybe because of sex," Chris said and they all remembered Olivia, a popular girl who'd had an affair with The Willing chaplain and as a result, was removed from her position as student council president.

When the phone rang, Shirley answered it.

"Probably the front desk telling us to quiet down," Chris said, but Shirley shook her head.

"We've already discussed this," Shirley said into the phone. She wound a curl on her index finger. "Leslie, I just don't think it's fair to the rest of us."

As soon as she hung up Shirley said, "I told her we already agreed — no dates, no spouses, no strangers."

"She won't come without the date. I know her," Gail said.

"So let her bring the guy," Renata said.

"Her date is a woman," Holly said.

Renata sensed an old obstinacy returning. "So let her bring the woman," she said, but nobody was listening to her. She slipped back to the time she'd been left out of a phone tree — girl after girl calling the next on the list until the entire class knew they could shed their maroon uniforms and change into street clothes for a choir practice with St. Peter's, a boys' school nearby.

IN THE RESTAURANT, they ordered sausage-stuffed mushrooms, seafood paté, caviar eclairs. And then steak tartare, pasta with sweet red pepper sauce, veal scallops with sherry, shrimp with snow peas and Crab Imperial. As the magnum of white wine began making its way around the table, Carly talked about goals, asking if everyone felt they'd accomplished what they'd planned.

"Are we on our deathbeds or something?" Shirley

asked, but Carly didn't laugh. Renata wished she'd delivered the wisecrack; she was irritated by the woman who'd run for class treasurer twenty years ago and lost, and now wore a device on her back that blocked pain signals to the brain. Carly's small pinched face made Renata think of those corporate women commuters, stiff and ready for confrontation.

Renata was savoring a mouthful of Crab Imperial when the waiter told Gina she had a phone call. Gina apologized and, as soon as she was out of hearing range, Holly said, "Probably that husband of hers."

"Maybe something happened with one of the kids," Renata said. While she couldn't imagine any situation that would make Lou call her, she couldn't envision maintaining control over a houseful of children either.

"And he couldn't handle it? He's a doctor, for God's sake," Shirley said. "He's checking up. He did it three times the afternoon she came to my house to visit."

When Gina returned, her face was flushed and she excused herself again. "What a jerk-off," she said, and Meryl immediately signaled for more wine. "We got married because I was pregnant and I don't think he's ever going to let me forget it," Gina said, a little teary-eyed.

BACK IN THE SUITE, where they watched a video of Gina's 140 acres, brick colonial house and riding ring, Renata had to smile. If her old classmates could only get a load of some of the places she had lived — squeezed into studios, a trailer, a sixth-floor walk-up, the apartment over the dog groomer's. . . .

As she watched Gina's daughters running through the pillared home, she began to feel lightheaded. In sixth grade, Gina had led her into what was called the cloak room, a small room of hangers and hooks and steel-gray lockers. Gina left the lights off and closed the door. Renata had obediently sat on Gina's lap after they'd taken off their clothes. She remembered the rectangle of light from the high cellar window illuminating their young bodies and how they had touched each other's tiny breasts and marveled at the dark lines sprouting beneath their arms and between their legs.

"I'm ahead," Gina had whispered.

Now as Shirley poured wine and Holly cut huge pieces of Frederick Willing cake, decorated with a pink-and-yellow insignia, a variation of the school colors —gold and maroon — Gina turned off the VCR and found an oldies station on the radio. They started a list of everyone's name and address. Renata saw that she was the only married one not to have changed her name.

Holly opened the door a little out of breath and flanked by two men in suits. "Hey, gang," she said, "this is Tom and Ron. I told them we needed a little assistance with the cake." Holly handed Ron a knife and told him to take what he wanted. The men, part of a convention of top-selling life insurance salesmen, had helped her to her car with the Tupperware containers.

Ron stared at Holly while he ran his middle finger across the frosting on his piece of cake. "Great," he said after he'd licked his finger.

Carly turned the radio up. "Wasn't this the best song?" she called over "Mercy Mercy Me".

There was a knock on the door and two more men showed up. "We heard there was a little party going on," the taller of them said. Renata recognized one of the men from the large table not far from theirs in the dining room.

"Cake?" Holly offered.

Ellen bent into Renata. She was a little drunk. "Let

me tell you a secret," Ellen said, but in a voice over the volume of the music. "I love my baby more than my husband. But, of course, I'd never tell *him* that."

Renata nodded. Meryl propped open the door of the suite because one of the men had started to smoke.

"Wow, it's like a mixer," Carly said when a few more men gathered in the hallway just outside the door. "Mixer" made Renata remember the large ball made of hundreds of pieces of mirror suspended above a dance floor. If you had taken your eyes off the guys for a minute and squinted in the dim light and swirling colors, you could have pretended you saw the sun, yourself part of an odd replica of the solar system, a moon or a ring or an undiscovered planet.

Renata saw Meryl go into one of the bedrooms with a good-looking man in a navy suit. She heard ice hitting glass, liquor poured. She wanted to feel anxious about what was going on all around her but she was giddy. Music poured from the radio into the smoky room where it sounded like everyone was laughing.

Someone took Renata's hand lightly. A man she'd never seen before.

"Look at that hair," the man said. "What do you do to it?"

"Not a thing," she said, "it's natural."

9
Toy Box

They sat at opposite sides of the tiny living room in Diane and Dale's apartment in Albany. The last time Renata and Lou visited, a glass-topped table had been centered in the room. Framed in macramé by Ren, the coffee table had been their wedding gift. Over the years, Lou had admired the pattern of tightly knotted cord and the loose-hanging threads, which moved with the slightest whiff of air. Hundreds of drinks had sweated and dripped against that glass top. A taco salad or a bowl of chips usually sat at the table's center, a brief diversion from conversation.

Today, the table had disappeared. Two wind-up swings, each rocking a twelve-week-old baby, stood in its place. At the base of the swings and around the sofa and chairs were strewn colorful blocks and interlocking forms, magnetic letters and numbers, cloth books opened on soft animal faces. The many rattles, balls striped and swirled with pastels, wooden trucks and the cars of a train, pieces of a plastic sandwich, Disney characters in different proportions made Lou dizzy.

Christopher, the three-year-old, wove between the twins' swings and along the ragged trail of toys like a miniature stuntman. The F.A.O. Schwarz teddy bear, outfitted in a beret and smock, which Lou had handed Christopher when they'd arrived, lay crushed beneath an ambulance at Ren's feet. The bear's smiling face was ground into the tan carpet.

Lou and Ren sat as if in a crowded nightclub, strangers. He thought about what it would take for him to distract Ren from the commotion going on all around them. To get her to look into his eyes, to captivate her with a witty remark.

They had arrived forty-five minutes earlier after a two-hour drive. It was their first visit since the twins, Jeremy and Justin, had been born. Lou remembered clearly the time they'd come to see newborn Christopher. A blizzard had forced them to sleep over with their friends. Dale had insisted. Diane said, "Don't waste your money on strange sheets."

They had slept on the new convertible sofa, its blue and gold plaid upholstery vibrant against the faded flowered wallpaper and frayed upholstery of the old furniture. "Let's break it in," Lou had said quietly to Ren. All day Lou had watched Diane flush with happiness as her baby turned and wiggled his little arms and legs on his yellow blanket. So ecstatic she couldn't concentrate on any conversation for more than a few seconds. Lou had studied his wife's face, too. Focusing on the baby, Ren had puckered her lips to soft coos and widened her eyes with amazement.

That night Ren and Lou made love without any precautions. When Lou had put his hand to her mouth to stifle her cries, he thought he smelled baby powder on his fingers.

Today, not a trace of that idyllic day survived when everything was pale — the snow at the windows, the baby's blanket, the sheets on the sofa bed. Today approximated a rerun of frantic scenes from Lou's youth. And he and Ren had no plans to stay over. Lou had rewrites for a new project and Ren was scheduled for an audition in *The Three Sisters*.

Diane reached over Christopher and pulled Jeremy from the swing. She pressed him to her breast. "I'm ashamed to tell you how rarely I get a chance to shower these days," she said, adjusting her blouse and shrugging her shoulders slightly. Lou averted his gaze from her breasts.

Diane looked proud that the three children demanded so much of her time. But Lou thought that motherhood had started to age her. Her long, tight ponytail was streaked with gray and her body had retained a noticeable paunch since the twins. The pale curves beneath her eyes, which had once brightened her expression, now made her look weary. Dale seemed exhausted as well, not debilitated, but as if he'd just played a doubleheader and won both games.

Christopher stared at his mother feeding Jeremy. Trying to get the baby's attention, he squeezed a plastic pig, then suddenly began reciting a progression of numbers. With his hazel, devilish eyes, Christopher resembled his father. At one time, Dale could surprise Lou with spontaneous suggestions for an evening at a topless diner or an outdoor theater a couple hundred miles away, or with his unique ideas on topics from car wax to existential angst. Lou wondered if this rebelliousness would manifest itself in Christopher.

The boy pulled up his shirt and said, "Me feed." Dale shook his head and smiled. "Kids," he said. Lou waited for him to go on, to relay an anecdote about Christopher, but Dale merely watched his wife feeding the baby. He looked in awe of her.

"Go ahead, let him take a crack at it," Lou said, but only Ren laughed. Lou had always been the group joker, making smart-ass comments in situations that demanded convention. When they'd all been working on a play together in New York City and the couples went out as a foursome, strangers confused who was with whom. Lou was dark and solid, a perfect physical match for Diane, while Dale and Ren had comparable lanky builds, softer features.

For a short time the four friends even shared a large loft in Soho. They all worked part-time jobs to support their theater aspirations — Ren and Diane were actors, Dale a set designer. Lou was the playwright who cracked jokes while the others cooked or cleaned or argued, his humor rescuing them from tense situations. Lou told himself that nothing in life was sacrosanct.

From the start, he considered Dale the most talented. Dale not only designed sets but painted in oils when he had time. But his talent and artistic vision hadn't been a strong enough support system. While Lou thought that Dale's bout with alcoholism ultimately drove him away from art, Ren professed that turning thirty had made Dale question himself and his profession. When Diane got a job teaching French at the State University at Albany, her hometown, the couple moved out of the city.

Dale explained to Lou the connection Christopher could make between the characters in his coloring book and real life. "Chris, who's this?" Dale asked, pointing to a large character wearing a hat crayoned green.

"Dr. Glow," Christopher answered, touching the picture.

"Dr. Glow's the pediatrician. He's fat and Chris saw him wearing a hat once when he left the office," Dale explained.

"Did he color this, Dale?" Lou asked of the stylistically filled-in wholes. To think that a kid so unformed could fit blues and reds to imposed limits was miraculous. A true indication of talent inherited. He held the book toward Ren but she was preoccupied with Jeremy.

"No," Dale said. "Diane did it."

"Oh," Lou said. He wanted a drink. A nice cold gin and tonic. But he felt uncomfortable asking now that Dale no longer drank. He was sure that Diane kept beer in the refrigerator because she'd mentioned that occasionally drinking one in the afternoon had a positive effect on her milk supply. But Lou didn't like to think of Dale handling the temptation of alcohol even from the refrigerator. And Dale wasn't offering; he was absorbed by the coloring book.

Diane held Jeremy on her shoulder and patted his back to encourage a burp. When Jeremy let go with a loud grunt, Diane praised him. As if on cue, Justin began to cry.

"Ren, would you mind holding this one while I get Justin?" She positioned the baby in the crook of Ren's left arm. The baby looked too big for his wife, Lou thought.

"I have to make a bottle for number two. My body just can't keep up with these guys," Diane said. Before the twins were born, during the last two months of her pregnancy, Diane had stayed in bed. Several times Lou had heard Ren comforting Diane on the phone. And afterward, Ren revealed that Diane said delivering two babies close to nine pounds each was the biggest accomplishment she could ever expect from her life.

"Your wife looks good with a baby," Dale said to Lou.

Lou glanced again at Ren, smiling at the now-contented infant. His wife seemed so much younger than Diane, than any of them. She put on a little makeup these days but nothing like what students wore to high school. And with her expressive eyes, she looked intriguing. Unworn, but not uninteresting.

Lou wanted to change the subject. But to ask Dale how his jobs were going, would mean pointing out a fact as painful as a physical handicap. Weekdays, Dale picked up blood and urine samples at various doctors' offices in Albany and delivered them to a lab in the center of the city. Three nights a week he worked as a short-order cook. Diane hadn't worked since two weeks before Christopher was born.

As Lou was deciding what to say, Dale yelled, "Christopher, put your shoes on."

"Dale, could you take this bottle for me?" Diane called simultaneously. "Justin just threw up."

"Here, Lou, could you help him?" Dale said, handing Lou a pair of black sneakers, a mini version of Dale's own.

While Diane and Dale were in the kitchen with Justin, Ren and Lou exchanged looks. She must have sensed how awkward he felt. He suddenly wanted to be with her. Just her. Somewhere — anywhere — else.

A bead of sweat from Lou's forehead dripped onto Christopher's sock as he tried to fight the little boy's foot into the shoe. Christopher began kicking his feet, daring Lou to grab one and segue into a game. The air in the room was thick and still except for the breeze around the kid's flailing legs.

"Well, I guess you'll want to have a girl next," Lou said, as Diane and Dale came back into the room. The couple looked at each other as if they'd just finished discussing this very issue in the kitchen.

"Dale, why don't you put on a little music?" Diane suggested quickly. Bobbling Justin in her arms as he squirmed, his face distorted in preparation for a wail, she asked, "How's *your* work going, guys?"

"I'm writing a movie of the week," Lou said, "and Ren's got a voice-over for Meow Mix."

"Fancy Feast," Ren said.

"That's great." Diane paused. "Actually, I meant theater."

"Fuck," Lou said with resignation. He thought he'd

said the word under his breath but Dale instantaneously covered Christopher's ears.

Lou didn't elaborate on the fact that he was writing for money now. He missed working with Off-Broadway actors, seeing the many copies of his play marked up and rolled and folded by the time the actors went off-book.

"I don't have the time for that anymore," Diane said. So Diane's acting had come to be called "that". Sometime when Lou hadn't noticed, maybe between Diane's waitressing jobs, or her visits to her parents in Albany, her need for acting had diminished. Lou wasn't sure. But ten years ago, they would have set down a bottle of Jack Daniels, not a damn lime seltzer, and had a rousing discussion about parental guilt that would have gone on till morning.

"Does it ever get frustrating. . . ." Lou asked, just as Jeremy let go with a high-pitched squeal. His swing had wound down. Immediately Dale stood up, turned the crank at the top of the swing. To Lou, it was an action that recharged not only the swing but the whole cluttered room.

Dale absently squeezed a goofy-looking plastic porcupine that wheezed as he spoke. "It looks a lot tougher than it really is," he said.

On the living room floor, Diane changed Justin's diaper and Dale changed Christopher's. Nursery rhymes played over and over in the background. Justin kicked hard at the air overhead, then as Diane was about to secure his diaper, let go with a high-arching stream of urine. "Oh no," Diane said, as she calmly washed herself and the baby and prepared him for a new diaper.

On the other side of the room, Christopher lay motionless as a stroke victim while his father undressed him. Diane explained how difficult it was to toilet-train boys. She'd even bought a kit with a bull's-eye that adhered to porcelain. Diane and Dale worked together, efficiently handing each other diapers and baby wipes and Vaseline. They synchronized so well that they could have been doing this baby business forever. Lou smelled feces overpowering baby powder.

"You see how it's done," Dale said to Lou. "Would you like to do the other little guy's?"

Lou just stared at Jeremy whining in the swing. Lou's arms were fixed to his lap. He couldn't move. Almost couldn't breathe. He couldn't even think of an appropriate wisecrack.

"Dale," Diane scolded her husband. "If you could just hold this one, Lou," she said, placing a clean Justin in his arms. "I can't keep track of who needs what." Lou looked at the infant staring back at him. The FM station was playing a slow, smoky saxophone solo but instead, Lou heard "Old McDonald," with the voice of Big Bird, on its fourth repetition. His head pounded. The scattered toys began to lose their definition and float into thick blobs. He turned his attention to Dale's sketches of theater sets, askew on the living room walls as if they were small doors to another, more desirable dimension.

Christopher, at large, grabbed the remote control channel changer. "Not now," Dale told his son. Christopher ignored him. Jabbed at the numbers on the changer. Dale grabbed Christopher's arm. "What did I say?" Grimacing, Christopher pointed the changer at Dale's face, pushing buttons defiantly.

In a breath that came out as a sigh, Dale said again, "Kids."

Lou set Justin in the swing and left the room. Smiled weakly at Ren when he passed her. In the bathroom, he could hear the faint voice of Cookie Monster. He searched the cabinets and hanging wire baskets. He bent over the sink and splashed water on his face. He wet the handkerchief in his pocket, pressed it to his forehead. Then he swallowed three generic aspirin.

In the bathtub, another pile of red, yellow, and blue plastic blocks and forms spread against the white porcelain. Lou thought of Dale's paintings, their geometric forms and strong colors, saw the images slipping off the canvas, transformed into primary-colored toys. Color and light and line, every technique that had been learned and practiced and revered by Dale, had ended up a fucking mess in the bathtub.

The faucet dripped when Lou shut it off. He counted fifty drips before he opened the door and walked through the kitchen back to the living room. Standing just outside that room, which now looked like a toy box the size of a garage, Lou stared at his empty seat, its scarred arms, at the dirty Venetian blinds, and ragged rug. He asked himself if Diane and Dale were so different from his own parents. Lou had always thought it made sense that children learn something from parents' lives, if not to take a different direction then at least to make more money. There should be some progression from one generation to the next.

Lou swiped the wet handkerchief over his forehead but it was cool for only a second. His stomach hurt from the aspirin. Across from him, Ren was cleaning her sunglasses that she'd just retrieved from the playpen.

"So," said Diane, "we want to get down to see your house but I don't know when." She gestured around the cluttered room as if she'd have to transport the entire contents.

Christopher stood in front of his father, dropped his head into Dale's lap, and, in another minute, stuck his finger in his mouth. Lou heard the sucking noise the boy's mouth made against the finger, then the clicking of an empty swing.

As the swing came to a halt and silence permeated the room, Lou said, "All I can think of is a juggler who finally gets all the plates spinning at the same time." The stillness washed over all of them, water without the pound of surf. Lou looked at his wife and friends each holding a sleeping child. A few minutes of reprieve full of innocence and trust.

"This is what you should write about," Dale said suddenly, breaking the silence.

"A family picture," Diane said.

"With humor," Dale said.

How dare they suggest what he should write about? Let them write about it themselves, he thought. "Well, I guess it's time to go. You ready, Ren?" Lou said.

"Oh," Diane said, blinking rapidly, "I thought you'd stay for dinner. I've got chicken defrosting."

"We need to head back. I have to call the producer in New York before seven," Lou lied.

"Call from here," Dale said. As he spoke, the room seemed to come alive again, mocking the suggestion.

"I need my notes," Lou said.

When Ren stood up, Justin began to whine, then cry. Jeremy followed the leader. Not to be left out, Christopher attacked a castle made of blocks, kicking them into the chair legs, the radiator. Lou could still hear the noise when he and Ren finally got outside. The three-story building, peeling and cracked, leaned slightly to one side, just like the sketches on the living room wall.

"They're really into the parenting thing," Lou said. His remark sounded simplistic in view of the intensity of his feelings, especially his rage at his friends' suggestion of a domestic subject for his writing. Ren only zipped and unzipped her pocketbook.

"How about a cigarette?" Lou proposed.

"A cigarette?" she asked. They'd both quit smoking

five years earlier. She smiled at him, then pushed her lips out in a pout. Her T-shirt clung tightly to her breasts.

When Lou pulled into the parking lot of a restaurant south of Albany, he intended to simply buy a pack of Marlboros from the cigarette machine but Ren came in with him. A hostess asked them if they were planning to eat. Lou looked quickly at Ren and then nodded yes.

After the waitress lit a candle at the center of their table, Ren pulled a small mirror from her purse. "Let me see that before you put it away," Lou said. He ran the back of his hand over his mustache.

Lou ordered gin and tonics, shrimp cocktail and mussel appetizers. Glazed salmon steaks with wild rice. He and Ren ate and laughed and blew smoke above each other's heads. When Ren mentioned saving room for chocolate mousse and Irish coffee, Lou reached over and, with his fingers, wiped a droplet of drink from the corner of her mouth.

"Maybe they're happy," Ren said. After a second she added, "They seem happy."

"You're probably right," Lou said.

10
What He Told Me

M_y father said he had something to tell me. "I'll come down this weekend," I said, reaching for the Amtrak schedule between Stamford and Baltimore. I would reschedule my audition.

"Just a minute, Renata," my mother said when she took the phone. "No more cookies, Leroy. Not before DINNER," she hollered. The phone clunked on the table; her muffled footsteps beat across the gold carpet. Then she said, "Damn it, Leroy. I told you NO MORE."

She returned to the phone out of breath. After striking a match for her cigarette, she said, "I swear I don't hear him for three hours. But the minute I get on this phone he's into something."

FIVE BLOCKS AFTER WE left the house, I pulled over to the curb, put the car in neutral and asked my father, "Why don't you drive?" I suppose I wanted to test him, to determine if my mother's complaints were verifiable or if she was overly fearful, exaggerating how aging *might* transform him.

"What do I do?" he asked, staring at me.

"Dad, you put the car in drive and you go," I said, hoping.

"Yeah," he said after a minute, "you go." Then, carefully, he slid toward the driver's seat.

"Where do we go?"

"Anywhere you want," I said, worrying even as I spoke that this escapade was doomed.

"I can't remember the last time I drove," he said when I reminded him of a stop sign. "Has that damn sign always been there?"

Since Dad had given up his part-time post-retirement position of golf instructor at Twenty Pines Public Golf Course, he'd begun to lose the concentration that he'd always insisted was the key not only to a good game of golf but to any accomplishment.

In some of the incidents my mother described, Dad's behavior made a weird kind of sense — like the time he supposedly returned a rake to the next-door neighbor. He leaned the tool against Mrs. Peters' fence, went inside the house to say hello to her and to pet her dog, then proceeded to walk to the front door, lock it, and ask, "Are we expecting any more company or can we call it a night?" When my mother finally retrieved him and asked what he thought he was doing, he replied, "All these damn houses look alike."

"Dad," I yelled when he came dangerously close to the car stopped in front of us. The driver checked her rearview mirror at the squeal of our tires.

The night before in the dining room, I'd noticed a place mat on the floor beneath my father's feet. Mom announced Dad's concern that bugs would crawl up his pants legs while he ate. And posted next to the black wall phone in the hallway was a note in Mom's bold handwriting, "DO NOT call Howie. He's DEAD."

AT THE NEXT INTERSECTION, he stopped at the yellow light. I breathed deeply. When I was a kid, Dad didn't like to stop the car for anything. His goal even on the simplest errand was to reach his destination without pausing at a single traffic light or any obstacle. He often plotted an alternate course before he left the house, and although this routine might cost him extra time and miles, he would choose it because it required no interruption. He would duck up and down narrow one-way streets, some paved with bumpy cobblestone, in his effort to avoid "getting stuck".

If his present was snarled with distortions and half-remembered functions, his distant past was usually un-naturally intact. "I'll never forget the time my Pop didn't see that train. Just in time he got over the tracks. The milk bottles in the back of the truck rattled like a cold man's teeth."

When the light turned green, the car behind us honked. Oblivious, Dad continued his reminiscence. "It's a good thing he made it. Otherwise, I'd never have grown up and met your mother and had you and David."

As he began to recite, like a prayer, the names of all his father's customers from that long-ago time, I inter-rupted, "So what did you have to tell me?" Because he recounted so many stories, he must have sensed the need to justify every minute of his past.

"Tell you?"

"On the phone you said you had something to tell me. That's why I came down, Dad."

"Give it a little time," he said.

THE CONGESTION OF SIGNS, clothing outlets, restaurants and while-you-wait repair shops soon disappeared. The road stretched out before us with fewer and fewer distractions of lights and merging traffic, and enticements for saving money. Focusing on the road intently, Dad was now holding the wheel with growing authority.

"I don't know the last time I played golf," Dad said. "I think I'll head over to the course." Comfortable enough to take one hand off the wheel, he rested it in his lap.

"You said you had something to say to me the other night," I prodded. But my father looked straight ahead at the road, far off narrowing to a mere strip of gray. I wanted to hear something as intriguing as when Dad had revealed to David that he'd been married twice before Mom. My brother had taken Dad out to hit a bucket of balls at the local driving range. With no provocation, Dad had said his first wife was "an Oriental woman", his second "a blonde bombshell".

"I didn't think there was any reason to tell you," Mom had answered when I questioned her. She immediately went on to report how after driving less than a dozen balls with David, Dad thought he'd shot the full eighteen-hole course with Walter Cronkite.

Now HE WAS DRIVING the car at a slightly faster clip. Fields interrupted by three- or four-store strip malls flipped by.

"So how's your job in the big city?" he asked. Mom had told me last week that he'd said to her, "Didn't we have another kid besides David? Didn't we have a girl?"

"It's good," I said, not bothering to fully explain that voice-over work was really a series of jobs. "And I'm hoping to get a part in this new Off-Broadway play." I started a plot synopsis of *Greenland,* in which a native woman saw her family's traditional way of life threatened by a man from outside who had plans to destroy her culture with toxic waste.

When he didn't appear to recognize what I meant, I realized that what he expected of me was far from what I demanded of myself.

I thought about illusion. It felt as if Dad were playing a role, that he wouldn't turn in to the golf course at all but keep driving past the entrance, back to Connecticut, or to some state he'd never visited, like Massachusetts. I wanted him to be the old Dad living with Mom in the tidy, fourth-from-the-corner house where he soaped and rinsed his car and trimmed his lawn during the interim when he wasn't at work.

He signaled and turned smoothly into Twenty Pines. I suspected that we'd practice at the putting green the way he'd once prepared for a weekend golf match. If he wanted to actually play a few holes, I could caddy.

"Renata, I need the driver now. Can you find it?" he used to ask. I could distinguish the different clubs before I was as tall as the leather bag that held them.

Dad parked in front of the putting green. The new leaves on two distant weeping willows blew out into the sky soundlessly. "Dad," I said, recognizing that I was still asking things of him, still a daughter wanting. No matter how muddied his mind, he should know that I had come down immediately to hear what he had to say because I wanted to know more about *myself.*

Dad put his hand up as if directing traffic. "Renata," he said, his voice a mix of tenderness and precaution, "promise me you won't put the kids before your husband."

A wash of confusion slipped over me. I felt as if he were explaining about part of his own life that had been lost. He had said the same thing years ago when I was twelve and he was that husband.

We sat in the car in front of the putting green for a long time without saying anything else. Distant unrecognizable figures on the back nine swung and stroked and walked. A group of birds sliced through the sky.

Finally I said, "Well, Dad, you want to practice?"

"Let these guys play through." He indicated two men in their fifties about a hundred feet away.

"They're just putting," I explained. "We can practice, too."

"Shhh," he said, "the third hole is tricky here."

The man in the bright yellow shirt took a long time

lining up the shot, then sank his putt from fifteen feet away.

"Remember your hole in one?"

"Kids remember the damnedest things," he said, still looking straight ahead.

When I was four-and-a-half, Dad made a perfect shot on the par three fifth hole of this course. The newspaper clipping was still framed and stuck to the knotty pine wall in the basement, and the dusty relic commemorating the accomplishment — a miniature club leaning to the side of a hole, which could double as an ashtray — I remembered him bringing home, showing my mother. It seemed important to them then to determine exactly where they should put it. Dad would smile at the trophy and sometimes Mom would gently touch it, sitting on the top of the television.

I thought I remembered how happy they both were.

"The heavy fellah's playing a pretty good game," he analyzed, as the men putted into the flagged cups.

"Dad," I said, pleading with him to come back. He pursed his lips, thin like my own, put his hand to them and rubbed. When his hand dropped back to his lap, his mouth looked perfectly relaxed.

The men moved on the impeccable green and joked as one after another of the dimpled white spheres plunged into its proper hole. Dad and I watched, mesmerized by the separate balls retrieved from cups and hit again and again.

Then the man in the bright shirt raised his putter high above his head, not in triumph but anger. He brought the club down sharply in front of him, the metal appearing to sink deep into the lush ground. The man remained bent over the club, shaking his head. The other man, holding his club parallel to the ground, kept his distance.

Dad turned to me. "All you have to do is keep your eye on the ball." He patted my hand, looked off. "Just remember that."

11

Renata's Resolution

I won't ever look for you in the eyes of a helpless crea-
ture. Won't color a name with gooey nonsense and chant
it with you behind me, chin resting on my shoulder, staring at tiny features that don't belong to either of us,
though relatives are sure to divide them up. I won't touch
delicate new skin, slide my finger along creases and
dimples of chubby leg and arm, leg and arm, brush my
hand across the fuzzy beginnings of hair and tiny start of
nails so often that I have no need for *your* softest spots.
Your hands intertwining mine in a fleshy knot. I won't
touch anything that could make me give up squeezing the
back of your neck, the curve of your shoulder, kissing your
knee and running that kiss up to the top of your leg. I
won't.

MY FIRST MEMORY is of the cat across the street that abandoned my caresses for two gray tiger kittens of her own. As
soon as she produced her litter, I found the cat repulsive.
I couldn't bring myself to pet her again.

I WON'T ECHO MY mother's frustrated screeching. And I
don't want a brood to buffer me from failures or details of
our own youth. And I never want to break into your con-

versation to say, "I'm talking to your father, sweetie." "Just a minute, honey." "Not now." "Not now."

I couldn't watch our replicated gestures spread into a family portrait so large that I'd no longer be able to put my arms around the crowd that attached itself to me. I couldn't apologize for every disruption, every obnoxious outburst with the word "tired". I hope I couldn't look for excuses so often that I'd become an excuse myself.

I'M NOT PROUD of my unnatural attitude. Sometimes I pretend to be when I stand before questioners empty-handed. Lap unfilled. Dress and hair untugged. While they blather on about fulfillment. New never-before-felt emotions. New fear. More important than anything. Almost holy. Better than sex.

They'll say, oh before the kids what a time we had. They'll say this with a smirk that means, but we've grown up.

I know that once you've given up alcohol, you never appreciate the taste of any liquid again.

LIVES GROW SIMPLER as the children grow up. School, TV, telephone, with interruptions of food. Hit Replay, turn the page. At the mall, the lanky adolescent babies loping ahead or behind, hanging their heads forward like they're on a long leash to nowhere. Meetings, games, tournaments, obligations. Get up, suit up, show up.

Parents say they believe in principles. They mean childlessness is a disease, something they've been cured of.

Children are a power greater than themselves.

I WON'T RETURN to you twelve or fifteen or twenty years later as if we'd been on a long trip to opposite ends of the same island, and say, "It's me. Remember?" And watch your sad, resigned smile searching for, Yes.

We'd be like prizefighters past our prime, punch-drunk, dizzy, afraid even to whisper, "Was it worth it?" lest we fall hard, bone-shattering to the mat.

THEY WILL HAVE the children and grandchildren and the continuity as tokens that once they loved each other with a purpose. Once they looked like these young athletes. Children will keep photographs, repeat adages, voice curiosities about the past.

You and I will have none of it. And how we hold each other, sleep so close not a piece of paper could slide between us, no one will ever know. I promise.

I promise I'll try not to let your body seduce me to prove what's between us.

12
Peak

Leah Jackson ran her hand along the top layer of fresh bedding, then repeatedly struck at the pillow's underside, her firm, methodical gesture forming a furrow in the spread. After she finished making the first bed, she moved toward the other. She was preparing for weekend guests.

Before her sons left home, their bedroom was a disheveled mess of clothing and shoes and computer paraphernalia, most of which she never really understood. They'd slept with their legs hanging over the beds' edges. Occasionally the boys had appeased her by pulling the spreads loosely over the crumpled bedclothes, creating the impression of hidden bodies. She missed the boys and the way they energized the entire house. But, in a way, she liked the bedroom better these days — neat and tidy as a real guest room.

Just beyond the window, Leah spied her huge pumpkins, now planted more out of habit than for eating. All the time spent chiseling at the meat, chopping and cooking, didn't seem to produce a tastier pie than one made with canned pumpkin from the supermarket. The first year she and Doug had grown pumpkins, the vegetables had swelled to an enormous size, larger and heavier than either of their young sons. She'd photographed the babies propped against the pumpkins.

From the doorway she surveyed the room all ready for Renata and Lou. A distant mountain tinged with the burnished reds of fall hung in the window like a painting. This weekend was peak — Vermont's fall foliage at the height of its splendor.

These beautiful weeks almost justified her life in the same state, same town. With the boys no longer demanding her attention and Doug often leaving her alone to pursue his own interests, she finally had the time to appreciate the value of her daily routines. She was forty-nine and assumed most trouble was behind her.

Leah heard Doug answer the door and allowed him a few minutes to greet their guests before she stepped into the living room. The more sociable of the two, Doug was quick with conversation and jokes while she preferred handling the physical details of entertaining. They'd lived with each other long enough to choreograph such situations without a spoken direction passing between them.

Renata's features had softened over the years. The pattern of gray in Lou's hair and beard made him look authoritative and wire-rimmed glasses complemented the mature image. Renata smelled exotic when Leah embraced her. The khaki-colored pants and silky scarf made Leah think of glossy magazine ads, so unlike her own image when shopping Vermont chain stores in an oversized top and sweatpants.

Doug opened a bottle of Merlot. Renata immediately revealed their itinerary through the colorful New England landscape, a surprise birthday gift from Lou. Leah remembered the young Renata as too shy and self-conscious for a would-be actress, well-meaning and determined but much too quiet.

When Renata had bought cider from Leah's father's apple orchard and mentioned that she was acting at the local playhouse, Leah immediately said, "Well, you must know Lou. We saw his play *Local Rites* last summer. He even came out afterward and shook hands with my boys." Leah liked that Renata talked to her, not indirectly via her sons as most shoppers did. By the end of the month, Lou and Renata were visiting the apple stand together. Renata winked at Leah as she and Lou bought apples and cheese and a loaf of Leah's homemade bread. And the day before their departure, Leah and Doug had the couple to dinner. Leah didn't normally exert herself socially but she'd been impressed by Lou's courtesy to her boys. That was what she'd told Doug.

Why were Renata and Lou really visiting now anyway? Leah received yearly recaps of the couple's activities with a holiday card but never a phone call until last month when Renata had asked outright if she and Lou could spend the day and night with them.

"So how are the boys?" Lou asked. Leah noticed that Lou didn't look at Renata as he moved the conversation onto the children.

"Josh is involved in about a hundred different things at college," Doug volunteered.

"Girlfriends?" Renata asked.

"I'm sure," Doug said and took a swig of wine. "But you know kids. He's mum about that stuff."

"Andrew's with a very sweet girl," Leah said of their older son, who'd dropped out of Dartmouth, where she and Doug had encouraged him to apply.

"Faith," she said, giving the girl's name, but not the fact that she weighed close to two hundred pounds.

"Andrew's making twenty-four dollars an hour as a computer consultant," Doug offered next. He didn't mention that Andrew seldom worked fifteen hours a week.

"That's terrific," Lou said and he seemed to mean it.

Leah never thought of her sons as failures until someone started asking questions about them.

Doug asked the couple about work and Lou replied that he didn't want to jinx his current project when film possibilities were so easily tossed into a southern California trash can. Renata was about to go into rehearsal for *Look Back in Anger.*

Even though she was pleased that she'd played a part in introducing the couple, Leah had told Doug at the time that such a marriage was never meant to last. She expounded on the theory so frequently that Doug finally told her to drop it. And she had, but she'd never stopped thinking about it.

She and Doug had had an orchestrated courtship. Leah had known Doug in high school, dated him when he'd gone to Meriden State College in New Hampshire less than an hour and a half away. During their two-year engagement, not one day went by that Leah didn't plan some detail of her wedding — the flowers, the flower girl, the rings, the perfect dress and shoes. She hadn't thought of herself beyond that celebration.

Doug was telling Lou about a nephew who'd joined a pyramid scheme and made $12,000 in three weeks from an initial $1,500 investment.

"Jerry came to me," Doug said. "He asked me if I wanted to be an entrepreneur, too."

"An entrepreneur," Lou repeated.

"'It's against the law,' I told him," Doug said. "He told me it's only against the law because the government doesn't have any way to tax it."

"It's definitely a gamble," Lou said and finished his wine.

"Leah, do we have any of those little crackers?" Doug asked. The night Jerry had called to tell them he'd made his way to the top of the pyramid and "cashed in", Doug hadn't looked at her. He'd put his head back and stared at the ceiling and wondered aloud if there wasn't something to Jerry's latest scheme. But Leah had told him, "Don't even think about it."

When Leah reentered the living room with a platter of crackers and cheeses, she saw that Renata and Lou had arranged themselves on opposite ends of the couch. And during Doug's next story, this one about finding his mother's bathroom drain clogged with thirty years of body powder, the couple nodded and sipped their wine but not in synch. In their early days together Renata and Lou hadn't been able to keep their hands off each other.

Leah wondered if she could have retained her desire for Doug if she hadn't had the boys or if indeed the children had rescued her from what she'd already lost. She wasn't sure she'd ever seen real passion in Doug's eyes, not even *before* they'd married. In many ways the boys had sucked them dry and now she and Doug, while they generally agreed on most issues, seemed to brush by each other on their way to bed or meals. She wasn't positive that agreeing was always the best thing; just last month she'd read an article entitled, "How a Good Argument Can Improve Your Sex Life".

"So, Leah, are you keeping busy?" Lou was talking to her.

The question made her a little defensive. She hadn't worked professionally since the boys were born, except for the family fruit stand at high season. Doug's job with the Green Mountain Power Corp. covered them comfortably, at least until the year they'd come up against the boys' simultaneous college tuitions. These days she had her garden club, her book group. She merely nodded at Lou and began dinner preparations.

Alone in her kitchen, Leah sliced vegetables, then discovered that the shrimp she'd prepared for an exotic Chinese dipping sauce smelled a little off. She delved into the freezer for some chicken, then ran it under tap water to defrost, her fingers growing painfully cold handling the frozen flesh. Because she hadn't even bought the shrimp on special, she couldn't imagine why they had gone bad so quickly.

Renata joined Leah at the sink. "This looks fabulous," Renata said of the colorful piles of vegetables. "I almost forgot what a terrific cook you are."

"I wanted it to be different," Leah said, meaning unusual. After all, her guests now probably ate at expensive restaurants on both coasts. Leah wanted to apologize, to say the meal could have been better with the shrimp, but instead she asked, "How's the house?"

"Expensive," Renata said. "The mortgage is astronomical." Leah and Doug had five years left on their mortgage, just over $100 a month.

Leah paused, unsure what to say next. She remembered the dinner she had made for Renata and Lou at the end of the summer after they'd met those many years ago. Later, even with the children sleeping nearby, Leah had been lustful. It was the first and only time she had initiated lovemaking in her marriage. She credited that experience to Renata and Lou's romance.

When Leah finally called everyone to dinner, Doug was showing Lou how to use his camcorder. "Lou's in the movie business, Doug," Leah said and feigned a laugh.

Doug filmed her as he moved out of the kitchen. While she tried to pose for the pictures Doug was sure to replay after dinner, she felt herself scowling.

The four passed plates and drank another bottle of wine. Leah wondered if Renata and Lou were recalling that dinner that was so vivid in her own memory. The couple hadn't stopped looking at each other long enough to sink a fork into Leah's specially prepared lake trout. Even without the shrimp, today's meal was a hit. It didn't have to compete with exchanged glances or feet entwining under the table.

Watching Renata eating gracefully, Leah wondered if she had had any affairs. Didn't actresses always fall in love with the leading man? She wanted to ask how the driven young woman had directed her life. Did Renata now look at Lou the way Leah saw Doug — an appendage of herself that excited her no more than an arm or leg? But Leah was no more effective with questioning her guest about sex than she'd been with her own sons.

After dinner the couples took a long walk down the country road, then crossed a meadow flushed with sunset and tiny white wildflowers. The luscious reds and yellows dropped all over the ground and floated in the sky. But as the sun disappeared, the fallen leaves made Leah consider that the world could use a good sweeping up.

At the house Renata went around to the backyard. "Do you still grow pumpkins?" she called. What had once amazed Leah — the growth of the squashes in such a short time — now almost sickened her. The bulbous orange growths hanging onto withering vines made her think of tumors. And when she prodded them, turned them so they'd color evenly, she became annoyed at their dead weight. Traditions, she thought, sometimes became rituals practiced solely out of fear of change.

That night in bed Leah said to Doug, "I think they're going to separate." The full moon lightened her pillow.

"Lou didn't mention anything," Doug said. He turned on his side to face her.

"Well, Renata didn't exactly either."

"Where are you getting this idea then?"

"I think that's why they came to visit us, to let us know they're breaking up." Because I brought them together, Leah said to herself.

"They'll tell us if it's true," Doug said and flipped onto his back. "Maybe they just wanted to visit us," he said sleepily. "To reminisce."

She knew that if he hadn't started snoring then, his next words would have been familiar ones — that she thought about things too much, that most people didn't have her sense of responsibility. That she hadn't gotten the couple together. They would have met anyway in their summer theater work. Still, stating her theory made Leah feel better than she had in months.

The next day after the guests had left, Leah went to the boys' room to strip the beds. She didn't pause to notice the spectacular reds and new clay colors at the window. She stared at the beds.

They startled her at first, like suddenly coming upon an accident. The one bed used, the other left exactly as she'd readied it the day before. It wasn't that either Renata or Lou had made one bed impeccably, the other left hers or his undone, the usual different halves of a marriage. No, the couple had squeezed into one bed that was too short and narrow for one of Leah's sons.

The mass of intricate folds in the layers of rumpled bedding brought a nest to mind. Leah bent and sniffed the wrinkled sheets. What Renata and Lou had left behind made her catch her breath, and she shuddered at such intimacy in her own house.

13

Hollywood

They'll hear about you. Your hands coarse from years of manual labor; your accent, fascinating because it's authentic New York; your ideas, especially those alarming ones shaded with humor. They'll want you.

Sleek black limos will idle in your driveway hours before your plane's scheduled to depart Laguardia. Soon, they'll tell you, all this won't be necessary. They'll say that before long you'll be living among them. In their town. Hollywood. Every time the limo leaves, the crushed stone driveway will resound with your past breaking apart. Watching your wife waving from the porch, already you're a part of a sappy B movie.

The phone won't stop ringing. You'll be invited to parties, at which the guests, unless they are stars or because they are stars, will function as human hangers for current fashion. Drinks, crisp pastries full of flavored air will circulate as names are spoken, decisions made. You won't overhear, "We want to green-light this picture," without hoping it refers to you.

Although you'll be warned about caffeine and cholesterol and body fat, your choice of coffee — black coffee — will astound them. They'll feel confident that, in you, they've found an original. You won't let on that whenever you gamble, say at Atlantic City, you always drink black coffee.

Your chest will feel broader than it is, your hands bigger.

Your hotel will have an outlet for more gadgets than you've ever owned. Your room will be equipped with five phones, one just above the toilet. The jeans you send out to be cleaned will come back with creases.

You'll sense a thin, strong net hammocking you just above every personal need. And yet nobody will mention money. That's what agents are for.

You'll know that the most outrageous thing you see or hear has been heard or seen before by another playwright. But, for the time being, you won't care.

You're not an actor but you'll play one in the producers' offices. Always you've tried to tell people what they want to hear — you've discussed football with athletes, talked yourself down in front of people stricken with tragedy. You won't know how to judge the movie people, what lies behind their non-corrective, colored contact lenses.

You'll start out with a prepared routine, get it down, even to the hand gestures as you weave through plot points. Those who are most interested will raise a finger for a glass of Evian, sit back and ask if you've discussed this idea with anyone else. And, without missing a beat, you'll say no because there's no other answer, and then slide right back into the description.

Every reference they'll try to explain, every question they'll ask you will be in terms of other films. In a twenty-minute meeting, you'll hear more films named than you've seen in ten years. Disparate films will jam up against one another to make a point. "It's a *Thelma and Louise* slash *Kiss of the Spiderwoman* kind of picture."

When you get bored with your pitch, you'll deliver a new idea, one that comes to you between appointments when you brake your subcompact rental car on the Santa

Monica Freeway. You'll try it out on a couple of studios even though you won't have thought it through to a satisfying, yet open-ended, conclusion. One of the studios will love the idea, pass it on to the producer who will take you to dinner. And you'll think, "This is *so* easy."

The producer will set up a third meeting to introduce you to his sons who serve as assistant producers. The boys will be tall and lanky and, if not covered with layers of privilege, come off as dorks. Immediately the three will begin to act like family — confiding, teasing, arguing. Your wife will warn you they're used to picking up and putting down people like glasses of water. You won't imagine not hearing from them after today. You won't even envision Thanksgiving without them.

You'll repeat the title of your yet-to-be written movie until it becomes a chant, then only a sound, finally something like a moan. You'll moan at the phone so often that eventually it rings.

Your agent will announce that he'd like to try a new venue. He'll arrange appointments for you with television people. He'll tell you this is where the real money is. You'll have no idea what he means by real money but you'll follow his instructions more closely than you adhere to the outline for a script.

The television people will not only want you, they'll want you to want them. The secretaries who greet you at the studios will introduce themselves as Baby or Panda. The development people, a few years older, will be wearing dresses tight as sausage casing, yet dare you to glance at their individual body parts. You'll have trouble remembering the spelling of their ordinary-sounding names — Keren, Aimee, Jaine, Cathee.

They'll tell you to sit anywhere you like but you'll know that your choice among sofa, easy chair, straightback chair will be something they'll make a note of, an indication of how they should expect to deal with you. You'll have an urge to jump on the glass coffee table, stamp your feet, make a precedent of yourself. But, a second later, you'll be sipping a glass of highly carbonated, vaguely citrus water you didn't ask for.

In the course of the meeting, they'll mention so many made-for-television movies and sit-coms that conversation becomes a pop-culture video. In this new language, the names of episodic-dramatic shows turn to verbs. If you happen to mention Dobie Gillis, you'll get a collective stare that will convince you you're old enough to have fathered anyone in the room.

The few times they'll refrain from referring to other shows and dare to use actual life experience to make a point, you'll detect an awkward grin spreading across your face. You won't be able to control it. You'll hear remarks that people back home are sure to think you've invented. A twenty-something woman announcing that she can identify with the homeless because, as a kid, she slept in her backyard two nights in a row.

To argue an idea, you'll present your original deduction that your cat believes you control the weather: if she wants to go outside when it's raining, she merely stands in front of the open door and rubs insistently at your legs the way she does when she's hungry, putting you in charge. The others at the table will be leaning forward, concentrating on you as if you've just stepped out of the Far East with a new philosophy for living well and hurting less.

You'll be required to arrange meetings around people's commitments to rolfing or fasting or individualized child care. Walking into sleek glassy buildings, you'll find your way to offices where crystals serve as paperweights and fat white rabbits hop between desks. You'll notice everyone yearning to be different but all tied to the same thing. Money.

Unknowingly you'll pitch a sit-com idea to a producer whose friend has died the night before. He'll stop you midway through the presentation to cry. You'll offer to return at some more appropriate time but he'll insist that you go on. After an agonizing half hour of trying to be funny, stopping to allow his emotions to catch up, then continuing on with one-liners, you'll watch him settle into a flurry of note-taking. His pen will continue to scratch against the pad of lavender paper well after you've finished talking.

Some of your ideas will be accepted for development. Although you'll want to work on the projects at home in Connecticut, the studio will coerce you into spending a few days with them to be sure you're moving in the right direction. Baby or Panda will visit your office intermittently with "How are you doing?" "Can I get you anything?" "Can I get you *anything*?" In the hallway, you'll swear you hear Baby or Panda ask, "I forget. Is Paris the city and France the country or is it the other way around?"

The development people will take you to dinner and tell you your ideas are wonderful, but too off center. With a few deft computer strokes you'll learn to turn black men white, Jews into Italians. You'll return home to work on rewrites. You'll be happy to leave the spacious west coast where you feel like a strand of DNA under a microscope. All that you will want right now is this: dinner in the kitchen with your wife, a real conversation devoid of references to movies or TV, and the cat without a pandering thought in its head brushing by softly.

You'll write pilots and movies that never appear on television for reasons beyond your control — the stars/producers divorce; the parents of a child prodigy think your work is the wrong vehicle for their career; people whose preference in bottled water you've memorized switch networks. After finishing one project, you'll pitch yet another idea. This will go on until you feel you're on a constant job interview.

Sometimes you'll bring your wife out to L.A. on pitching expeditions. She'll attempt to distract you between appointments with sex, with food. She'll be trying to pull you back into your real self, softening your hair with her fingers, tracing your backbone rigid with tension and ideas, but you won't be able to feel anything, taste anything. All the while you drive the thruways of Southern California zigzagging into the breaks between traffic, you'll envy her in the hotel rooms waiting for you. You'll envy her until the moment you return and slide your card into the lock.

In one of your most memorable presentations, you'll arrange to meet a producer at the airport during the few minutes before his flight. He'll arrive late, out of breath. You'll stand a couple of feet apart just beyond the American ticketing lines. He'll listen to you, but before you've gotten through the first scene he'll look at his watch. He'll say, "Run with me."

And you will. As you jog to the appropriate gate, descriptions of character motivations will automatically pump from your mouth. He'll seem to nod or maybe that's only the impact of his running. You'll leap over a huge suitcase on wheels and a leash. He'll stop, thank you as he's shaking your hand, then run down the ramp on the final boarding call. You'll be standing by yourself, listening to the boarding apparatus purr and pull off. You'll try to remember his face as metal hits metal. You'll hear your heart pound against your chest for only a second before it's muffled by the engine roar.

You'll get fewer appointments and be assigned even fewer projects. When they say audiences won't be able to identify with your characters, you'll feel like you're in a destructive marriage. Someone will be trying to change you, rid you of the very qualities that were once the attraction.

You'll worry about joining too many of your peers who have left the New York theater for the west coast and yet you'll begin to think seriously about relocation. The weather will be beautiful.

You'll change agents. You'll change agents so many times that someone will finally say to you, "You've got it all wrong, Lou. In Hollywood you're supposed to have one agent, many wives."

The dreaded phrase "turn around" will be bandied about so often that it becomes your middle name. You'll fantasize floating over the film industry, forgotten scripts drifting around you like clouds. You'll grow as dark as the typeface of directions pressed across endless white pages.

In spite of this, or maybe because of it, you'll find yourself pitching L.A. to your wife, surrounding the city with positive adjectives. You'll try to convince yourself that proximity is the key to getting work. She'll maintain that elusiveness is the answer, as in romance. But not so elusive that they forget you're alive, you'll say. A good compromise might be Malibu, Manhattan Beach . . .

She'll listen but you'll be able to tell she doesn't buy your p-o-v for a minute. Not since they demanded that your black character turn white.

One evening when there's still the possibility the phone will ring with an enthusiastic voice, one of your ideas will turn up on TV. An idea that was rejected because although it was interesting, it had no precedent. Every TV producer needs the success of an earlier show to believe in your project, they told you.

The edges of the main character will have been smoothed down as if he's lived in an institution too long but you'll hear lines of dialogue that sound as if you've just spoken.

Your wife will say, "Hey," and look over at you. You'll see her ready to defend you, to tear into Hollywood with manic frustration. But you'll put your index finger to her lips. And hold her hand.

The two of you will sit in silence until the show is over, the credits roll by so fast you catch only every fifth one and you flick off the set like a snap of the fingers.

She'll say gently, "I know how you feel," and you'll tell her she has no idea how you feel.

III

Beyond Them

14
Baja

The afternoon Renata and Lou argued about moving permanently to California, it was raining. They sat on the balcony of the Sunset Grande Hotel in Bel Air and watched the rain and then the sun turn the grass a kelly green and intensify the colors of flowering bougainvillea. It was February and in Connecticut there was over a foot of snow.

Months earlier Ren had tacked a vacation in Baja, California, onto the end of Lou's business trip. That was when his assignment to turn the popular novel, *A Brief Business Matter,* into a television movie had seemed like a sure thing. Then, just the day before yesterday, the producer told Lou that the project had been shelved due to an unresolvable contract dispute.

In a funk over the canceled project, Lou had wanted to forget the vacation and return home immediately. But Ren pleaded for all her arrangements — plane from L.A. to Tijuana, the car rental at Tijuana, hotels all the way down the mission-strewn Baja peninsula to Cabo where they'd fly back to L.A. and then connect with a flight to Kennedy secured by their frequent-flyer miles. She said it was a small concession, considering she was thinking about the move to L.A.

While Lou's agent had been scrambling to make appointments with other studios for different projects, he had repeated his advice to Lou: "You really should think about living in L.A." More and more people had been encouraging Lou to move west for the best opportunities.

"No one's *promising* you work if we relocate all the way out here," Ren said, clinging to the last vestige of her harangue against the west coast. She hated its seasons, which were as indistinguishable as its ethnic influences, and loathed its emphasis on the "deal", which penetrated every social occasion. Renata knew her argument for staying in Connecticut and living among friends instead of business associates was wearing out just like the tires on their three-year-old Jeep. Each month the mortgage on their house was becoming more difficult.

"We wouldn't have to live here forever," Lou said, refilling their wine glasses. "I mean we could try it for a few years. We could rent our house." He paused. "I guess I feel this is my last shot, Ren." Lou was forty-three.

They'd bought their house in Connecticut five years earlier, two weeks after Lou received the check for *Cornered*. It had been the third house they'd looked at and both of them knew simultaneously that it was the right one. The dark wood interior of the house suited Lou and Ren admired the acreage of oaks and beeches at the end of a dirt road.

"Why don't we see if we *can* sell it?" Lou offered. He was thinking of the recession and the hard-hit New England real estate market. As they finished the bottle of Burgundy, they agreed to put the house on the market as soon as they returned home.

CHECKING OUT of the hotel, Lou remembered when he didn't have to use Sprint bonus points to get a free hotel room. He would simply sign his name and the name of the studio and that was it. That was back when everyone was courting the image of the rough-edged, new-found screenwriter. Before Rex Reed's televised comments about *Cornered,* which three different people called to repeat: "This movie is weirder than a two-headed calf."

Ren regretted her lavish breakfast as soon as she spotted the miniature plane for Tijuana. Besides Ren and Lou in the nineteen-seat prop plane, the only other passenger was a man wearing a cowboy hat wider than his headrest and carrying a metal attache case.

Before the pilot, who looked about seventeen, pulled a divider between himself and the three passengers, Lou noticed a Teenage Mutant Ninja Turtles sticker adhering to one of the controls. "Panic Button" decorated a dial on the far right of the console. Lou decided not to point out these details to his wife.

As the small plane rose and fell and shuddered with the slightest current, L.A. and its mounds of unproduced scripts the size of Studio City disappeared more quickly than Lou could have imagined. After a particularly severe dip, Ren straightened her index finger and pulled it quickly across her throat. She lowered her head toward her lap to stave off nausea and Lou rubbed the back of her neck.

Ren guessed that things could only improve — after the blow of Lou's project being canceled and this dicey plane ride — but she couldn't rely on it. For years, she'd been counting on Lou's work to pick up, his writing career to gain respect, his agent to place properties easily, the envy of friends to subside. She hoped this trip wouldn't be the next entry on their list of disappointments.

The next time she looked out the window, the sea was replaced by scrubby, dirt-colored mountains. Ren thought she heard laughter coming from the cockpit.

Lou tried not to reveal his concern. They'd been flying well over the scheduled hour. The pilot was probably lost. Lou didn't want to die now — a playwright/screen-

writer with no prospects. A guy who'd just coerced his wife
to give up her dream house in New England, planning to
scavenge for work in an industry where being over forty
put you in a special interest group.

THE HERTZ RENTAL CAR had been booked months in ad-
vance but it took two hours after Lou signed the paperwork
before a young man kicked the tires of an old VW bug.

"I don't know about driving this through the Baja,"
Lou said, pulling at his mustache.

"Are you kidding?" Ren said. "VWs are the most reli-
able cars going." They'd each owned a Volkswagen once
and Ren felt a surge of nostalgia as she loaded their bags
under the hood of the car the color of a dirty Coke can.

Driving through the midday traffic of downtown
Tijuana, Lou found himself on the horn or brakes constantly. Cars darted around him, stopped short in front of
him as fiercely as in Manhattan, only there at least he knew
where he was going. The narrow streets, overrun with
pedestrians and unattended young children, street ven-
dors pushing carts of food, produce, and crafts, were
impassable at points. Lou heard Spanish hurtling through
the air, mufflerless trucks backfiring and smelled meat
grilling, though he couldn't identify it as beef and his
body didn't register hunger. Positioned to one side of the
road, traffic lights weren't easy to spot. Lou went through
a couple of reds but so did other drivers.

"Jesus," he said. "This is a nightmare." In five minutes, the recent decisions — studio executives' to cancel
the project, a possible move to California — became suddenly abstract, metaphorical even, remote as an empty
concert hall to the teeming life outside the VW.

Beyond the city limits, Lou reduced his speed to a
crawl over mammoth drainage pipes only partially buried
across the road surface.

"Do you think we'll make it to the end?" Lou asked. They had over a thousand miles on Highway 1 ahead of them.

"We have to," Ren said succinctly. "We've got plane tickets. . . ." She paused. "On a regular-size plane," she said, rolling her eyes, "from Cabo back home." Ren decided she'd rather gamble on what lay ahead than return to L.A. in a joke plane piloted by a pimply teenager.

"I'd feel a lot better if I knew the gas gauge worked," Lou said. As they headed south toward Ensenada, a newly paved, four-lane highway suddenly appeared with the backdrop of the brilliantly sunstruck Pacific to the west. Intermittently, mansions were poised above coves to catch spectacular views. Ren noticed a stucco post-modern building with enormous skylights on the edge of a cliff. A huge spray of ocean rose above the road, above the house. "Top that one," she said, but before she could turn to Lou for a reaction, they passed a collection of huts and lean-tos made out of scrap wood and weathered particleboard. Next came broken-down ranches that looked like abandoned ghost towns, outfitted with satellite dishes.

Farther along the road another extravagant residence appeared and then another string of shacks that looked made of cardboard. These extreme designs for living in such close proximity made Lou think of his latest preoccupation — when was it exactly that the arc of his life shifted from promising to desperate? He decided that he must leave New England at once and move to L.A. to demonstrate his commitment to Hollywood. His availability.

THE NEXT MORNING it seemed obvious that Ensenada was the farthest most North Americans drove into the Baja. South of the city, traffic thinned out to a trickle, the luxury homes displaced by working ranches and barren roadside. The modern highway narrowed to a two-lane road.

Occasionally chilies planted on hillsides jolted the landscape with color but generally a pale shade of parched earth painted everything they could see. The monotone of road and buildings and open land hypnotized Ren until she had a flash of memory about the previous December when she and Lou had driven home from friends. Sated with food and good talk, they were comfortable in the warm dark car. The moon had been particularly bright, and when the snow started, bits of the glowing body appeared to flake off and drift onto the road. Renata mentioned that night but Lou ignored the comment and said, "Is there a map in the glove compartment?"

"Lou, there's only one road." She paused. "One or two."

"I want to get a sense of how far we've gone."

The road fell gracefully into a valley of vineyards, gradually rose again and then descended sharply to a sandy plain. An immense mountain towered to their left and to the right lay the Pacific and an array of volcanic cones. Soon they caught sight of the mainline of travel before the paved one was laid — a shadow of a road about the width of a riding trail. The old dirt path, which verified their way through the peninsula, reminded her that in the past travel was tougher. She surprised herself by announcing that she wanted them to venture onto the old route. Lou said the VW was sure to get stuck.

"Come on," she said, "it will be an adventure." She felt confident again, away from planes and movie studios.

"The main road is a big enough adventure," he said. He'd seen plenty of *despacio* signs to make him cautious. "Besides, you'd need a four-wheel drive." He spoke without taking his eyes off the road.

When the hills flattened out, Ren was reminded of the Louisiana landscape where *Cornered* had been shot. It had been over a hundred degrees there, too. Even at night, the air heated up to mid-day temperatures under the artificial lights. Most of the time, she had stayed in the hotel room or sat on its balcony and waited for Lou to finish rewrites or return from a stretch of shooting. She read books and practiced monologues but often grew bored. She seemed to have spent her whole life waiting — for Lou, for callbacks, for that part she really wanted, for someone — anyone — to notice *her.*

After stopping briefly at Hotel La Pinta for lunch, chili pepper sandwiches that Lou had mistakenly ordered in Spanish, Ren took over the driving. Staring ahead at the bleak but beautiful sand dunes, she entertained the possibility that *her* life could change in California. Over the stinging hot sandwiches Lou had said, "Look at Lisa. Three weeks in L.A. and she's queen of the sit-coms." And someone was always shooting a film, looking for extras.

Ren downshifted. The cardón cacti became larger and more numerous, like bizarre bodies from another planet. The cirios made Ren think of lashing whips. As the road continued to steepen, Ren could see the way ahead winding even higher. The VW hugged the mountain cliff, the narrow road unprotected by guardrails. Below them was nature, pure and wild and untouched. A ruin in black and tan. Dangerous.

"Take it easy here," Lou said. "Want me to drive?"

"I do," Ren said, her voice sounding shaky. "But there's no place to pull over probably until we hit Cataviña."

THE NEXT DAY Ren and Lou directed the red Volkswagen as it crested mountain after mountain and then descended to a dry lake, parched and cracked. Color, any color, defied the lifeless landscape. In the Vizcaíno Desert Ren felt the desolate surroundings had finally baked onto her, onto her skin and into her hair, that she'd become part of the terrain.

Just when her burned lips and dusty skin became excruciatingly irritating, the aquamarine of the Sea of Cortés appeared. Simply staring at the water gave Ren the relief of sipping a cool beer.

Their motel stopover was perched above a mouse-colored road that on the map was a mere pencil mark. The complex was backed against a bluff overlooking the sea. A large pool drained of water and badly in need of a paint job stood in front of fifteen units and a restaurant-bar with a dirty picture window. Ren remarked that the place could have been the setting for a '50s horror movie.

"It looks OK," Lou said unenthusiastically.

"Why aren't there any other cars?" Ren asked. She stopped to feed a bony tailless cat a packet of crackers from her purse. In the restaurant the Mexican who delivered iced beers had light red hair. He and the cook ate at the end of the bar after they'd served Ren and Lou. The way the men ate, keeping their eyes on Ren and Lou at the same time, reminded Lou of the cat, wary and slyly attentive. No one else came for dinner.

When Ren slid the window of their room partly open and then pulled the curtain shut, Lou asked, "Any more cars in the lot yet?"

"Nope," Ren said. The room was standard, clean if old — two double beds with brown and yellow print covers, beige tile floor, stone walls painted white, no TV. No phone. With nothing about the room distinctive or repulsive, Ren and Lou relaxed. The cat Ren had fed earlier sat just outside. When she cracked the door, the animal cried in a string of pitiful squeaks.

The warm night air was loud with insects. With the lights out and Lou snoring gently beside her, Ren considered how satisfying the road trip was now that they'd gotten into the pattern of it. Each day driving a little closer toward their destination, each day worrying only about eating and sleeping, and then taking the pleasures of cold drinks and good food and each other at day's end. Lou had agreed that in just two days he was thinking less and less about L.A. and their future and more about how far they'd driven in this country where few people did much more than survive.

Ren set the alarm clock to catch the sunrise but woke with a start at 12:30. The calm night was punctured by laughter not too far off and crackly radio music.

"What the hell's that?" Lou asked.

"That" sounded like a glass bottle rolling along cement. Two car doors creaked open. Then a third and fourth. Two slammed shut.

The Spanish voices moved off slightly and Ren gave into sleep again. In her dreams, she heard music that had been the opening soundtrack to *Cornered*. The atonal six notes trickled along her skin and out to her fingertips. But then the tempo speeded up and the Mexicans outside the room began singing to a tune that wasn't familiar at all.

"Do you think we could ask them to move a little farther off?" Ren asked. The staccato music, which Lou thought was probably a Mexican pop song, blasted across the motel complex.

"I don't think that's such a good idea," Lou said and Ren didn't press him. He looked out the peephole but couldn't see anyone.

Lou didn't understand the words to the next song either. The men were howling from the far end of the motel units. It wasn't mariachi, for sure. Though it was black in the room, Ren had her glasses on.

When the song was over and Ren sensed the laughter once again trailing off, she carefully got up and pulled the curtain back slightly. She spotted a twenty-year-old Buick with the back doors flung open, abandoned. Hanging there, they looked like the wingspan of a vulture she had seen earlier that afternoon. Not far enough away sat the little red Bug.

"I guess there's no complaining to the management," Lou said when the music started up again. "They well could be the management."

Ren thought of the red-haired man who'd served them beers. "Yeah," she said softly. "Maybe they'll pass out."

"I think we've heard this one already," Lou said as another chorus of howls began. Suddenly the music blared ten feet from their room. One voice screamed above the others in a jumble of Spanish.

"What are they saying?" Ren asked.

"Can't tell," Lou whispered, though he was fairly certain one voice had said, "I need a woman!" Lou thought of the band of dirt road, their car too close to the Mexicans for an easy getaway. He thought of the flimsy lock on the doorknob that even a kid could push open. He thought, we have NO PHONE.

"I think we'd better get dressed," he said.

Soon there was no more music, just men screaming at capacity. They hooted and yipped and yelped like wild dogs over a fresh kill, then abruptly went quiet.

Lou analyzed his belongings, trying to conjure a weapon — nail file, corkscrew.... He would break the neck of the bottle of wine he and Ren had finished before dinner.

Remembering the motel's promotional brochure promising picturesque tranquility, Ren giggled nervously. "Stay with me," Lou said gently. They were both on the bed fully clothed.

Someone was walking along the front of the motel trying doors. The rented VW would give Ren and Lou away. The footsteps shuffled closer. Ren held her breath as the doorknob to their room moved this way and that.

The tailless cat she'd fed earlier mewed with hunger. Sensing the man breathing just on the other side of the wall, Ren told herself that if she and Lou got out of this mess, she'd move anywhere in the world. She'd make no more comments about missing the seasons in New England or the New York theater.

Lou heard the doorknob tried again, more emphatically this time. The sound of glass breaking came from the far end of the complex and the man outside their room moved in the direction of the crash. Lou said, "I think they've broken into the bar."

"So they're not the management," Ren said, though that discovery hardly made her feel secure. "They'll pass out for sure now," she said.

Lou got up, found the empty wine bottle, struck it against a table, then lay back once more beside Ren. He held her hand and with his other clutched the jagged bottle. A nearby door being forced open gave him an odd sense of relief. At least the Mexicans weren't dropping the VW into the empty pool. "They're going to sleep it off," he said, as if he knew that to be true.

Ren tried to imagine the map, the outline of the Baja, that appendage of California, that broken-off, broken-down piece of Mexico.

When the alarm clock sounded, Lou immediately slapped it to the floor. He gently set the broken wine bottle in a trash can as if it were a remnant of a dream. Through the peephole he caught the welcome red of the Volkswagen, parked exactly where they'd left it.

Then the music and yelling started up once again. Lou looked at Renata, fearful, exhausted.

"What should we do?" Ren pleaded.

"Let's get the hell out of here," Lou said. The daylight made him braver. A rusty station wagon sat in the middle of a ring of empty cans and bottles. Three other motel room doors were open and broken glass trailed like water along the front of the motel. Lou kept a close watch in his rearview mirror.

FOR THE REMAINDER of the trip, as Highway 1 bent westward and into the interior, then crossed emerald agricultural lands that might have belonged to the Midwest, they didn't talk about the incident. In La Paz, their hotel had individual cottages, big fluffy towels and television. Ren suggested that Lou should probably call his agent. Instead, Lou drank too many beers at the bar and discussed his writing. She listened carefully as he explained that you start with your own experience. Then you make characters you can trust to give those experiences to. You change details. Eventually you forget what's really true. But it doesn't matter.

"Over and over you give your experience away," Lou was saying. "And that's a good thing." He took a hearty swig of the beer. She'd lost count of how many they'd had.

Finally, in Cabo San Lucas with its credit card signs and massive turquoise swimming pools, they felt they'd made a circle of their Baja experience instead of a ragged line south. Few people traveled the tough midsection of the peninsula as they had. Most preferred the comfortable ends.

Later that afternoon from the window of the VW, Lou pointed out land's end, where the Pacific and the Sea of Cortés met. The juncture was marked by a massive boulder, with an opening worn through its center from centuries of water hitting stone in the same spot. The image moved Lou though he couldn't say exactly why. He kissed Ren and said that he wanted to stay in New England. The decision made him feel as if some missing piece of his puzzle had fallen perfectly into place.

15

Intimacy

In theater, every motion is larger than life. Your face twists and stretches beyond ordinary expression until it hurts. Your arms embrace the stage, the brightly painted flats, the audience in the last row. Your voice bounces across the wooden flooring, past stage lights and along the surface of imagined water. There is no end to you. You can reach the farthest shore.

When I projected my characters onto an empty stage, even the theater intern preparing for intermission in the lobby could hear my cries of rage, sobs of resignation.

Once I played an Inuit woman carefully undressing for bed, in slow motion pulling off piece after piece of clothing as if each were a limb of her body. Seconds expanded into the air and held the audience in a motionless trance that seemed to last a week. When I finally stood totally naked in front of all those strangers, before I even spoke my lines or the lights went down, my body overran the edge of the stage. It felt as huge as Greenland.

When I was younger, when I first kissed on stage, the moment was nothing like my own first kiss in the back of a Firebird. On stage I felt my theatrical gesture was a responsibility that went beyond two pairs of open lips. The imprint of my parted mouth made a hole the size of a forty-one-inch projection TV. Any of the other actors could have fallen into it.

I plunged into character after character. I've been so many different people that at times I've sensed myself hauling around every known neurosis and psychosis, costumed in layer after layer of disguise until I wore the stifling wardrobe of Everywoman.

Coming home after a week crammed with rehearsals full of another person's character, I couldn't eat an apple or a piece of toast. Basically that is how I've kept my weight under control. The play is my professional trainer.

"Actress" isn't a word anymore; it's "actor." But I've been in the business long enough to know both; I've been both. I've known the designation that conjures up a frill along the lower half of the body, a scalloped edge, the tail feathers of a showy, flightless bird. And I've performed in black leotards that swell and recede with the body form, that hide nothing, accentuate nothing, that say, This is what female is beneath the lace, the ruffles. Nothing's hinted at, nothing flutters in coy suggestion about obvious sexuality.

People not involved in the theater think it's a little crazy to take on some other person's psyche every night. What can it be like, they've asked, to make a career out of becoming other people, writers' visions, instead of polishing your own self into the glinting gemstone? But acting is not like *losing* your sense or your marbles. It's not substituting another person for yourself. What you do is add the other onto the essence of yourself. You learn to accommodate yourself to characters you live inside, even for the briefest audition.

Between shows, between tryouts, there's the waiting. My real life's full of pauses that an audience never sees. Anticipating the phone to ring with a callback, I've done more waiting than acting over the years. And yet, during the quiet times, expectation hasn't shrunk to withering self-doubt. It's filled every corner of every place we've lived.

With every birthday, there are fewer roles for women. Somehow, over the course of my struggle with artistic destiny and the need to eat, I've become a voice apart from a body. In voice-overs I'm the words of enticement, not the full-bodied enticement of the stage. I represent a recommendation of or reaction to the bowl of cereal, the spotless glass. I'm neutral, sexless, giving advice like the girl next door you've known since she was a baby.

At what point does a person stop and question, am I overweight? Two pounds, twenty pounds, two hundred? Sometimes I feel like a helium balloon Lou takes with him everywhere. I idle above his head, calling attention to myself as a useless spectacle while he makes impressive talk below me.

For Lou, the turning point might have been when the movie cameras started rolling over his plays, spreading manure into the white spaces around his stage directions. At first he wrote characters whose dialogue captured a live audience, compelled them to laugh back, filling the house with spasms of release. With film, directors focus on faces, close-ups impossible on stage. What the slightest squint of an eye can impart in a movie requires hyperrealism in front of a live audience. And on tape everybody wants a happy ending, small and succinct enough to tuck into a pocket for the ride home. No big questions, the kind that can drip out of suitcases and drag along the ground to the next destination. The house painter in *Blue Corners,* the play, who wants to paint the world white becomes only a face with a goofy hat in *Cornered,* the movie. Five brush strokes replace his moving monologues.

I've never acted in one of Lou's plays. I would like to have played the lead in *Daily Life* or maybe the wacky sister-in-law in his one-act, *The Gift,* both written and rewritten less than five feet away from me in the kitchen. What if we *had* joined forces, committed ourselves to the talent that each of us admired in the other, gambled our relationship the way we took every other chance? *That* could have made a difference.

We had both agreed long ago that even routine technical judgments could be skewed by our emotional involvement. Artistic competitions could grow to dangerous proportions if we tried to squeeze a theatrical collaboration into our marriage. Then we hadn't counted on my role diminishing to a three-word promotion for hair color or the guilt of Lou's main character abridged to an eye spasm.

Lou was losing faith in the breadth of his monologues. If I recited another woman's lines in bed, he easily picked them out, put his hand over my mouth. Our double bed, our own private arena, shouldn't become a stage, need to hold an audience.

It's a sanctuary from the business.

So now we shrink into each other.

Sheets flung over us are like nets keeping us together away from the world.

Instead of props we use fingers and hands and lips. Instead of words, we moan and shriek. Instead of song and logic, we are muscle. Our legs become two legs, our heads one head. We pound and press and squeeze our way closer until nothing matters but oneness. And sweat.

Professional ambition may seem like a burned-out bulb. But after sex, after we break apart, even when the male member recoils from a condom, that's not the end of *our* light.

16

Commitment

Just before the valet took their eight-year-old Nissan and followed a BMW into the parking area, Lou grabbed a tie from the glove compartment. Renata helped him adjust the purplish strip of silk as they headed toward the ivy-covered Tudor castle.

Mingling with guests in the courtyard, Ren would never have guessed the gathering was a wedding. A movie screening maybe. The guests and bridal party were almost entirely industry people — producers, directors, writers — many from the west coast. Of course, she hadn't expected this wedding to be anything like the ones she'd attended for friends in Baltimore. At those celebrations, each one exactly like the last, you couldn't walk five feet without mentioning the bride. Ren would have welcomed a couple of words, even a snide comment, about the woman of the moment; she didn't know anything about Suzette.

Someone going on about "a lasting story" was the closest to appropriate wedding lingo, and that referred to a foreign film in which a boy's life was transformed by the movie theater in his hometown. Then she heard the groom's name mentioned — Richard — the fifty-five-year-old producer who'd commissioned Lou to write a script that was currently in the holding tank between production and release.

Ren watched her husband nervously plucking at his

tie, an article of apparel he seldom wore. "At least it's close," she said. The drive into Westchester County had taken less than an hour from Connecticut.

"If it had been in L.A.," Lou said, "we wouldn't have gone."

Ren looked sideways at Lou. With all his unrealized projects, he was becoming more and more hard-nosed. Each time logistics fouled up or promises failed to material-ize and some toady called with the bad news, Lou lost some of his enthusiasm for the next script doctoring. Ren contin-ued to hope, coaxing Lou as well as herself not to give up.

As Lou moved among fellow writers and nodded to directors and was introduced to other producers, Ren accustomed herself once again to the periphery. Once in a while, someone would say, "Don't I know you from some-where?" or "What's your name again?" But few people from Hollywood cared about her still-small parts in the theater. With them, the stage existed only to segue into movie development.

Ren thought of her brother, also on the fringe of the movie industry. A driver for the cast and crew of Barry Levinson's Baltimore movies, he'd told her just last week that he'd be playing a SWAT team member in a new John Waters comedy. David hadn't sounded overwhelmed about being an extra, just glad for the additional pay from his brief appearance. Ren understood her brother's reac-tion perfectly. Hovering around the movie world was more chore than glamour.

She listened to the writers, Lou among them, talking about their scripts. Most of them were working on spec, on promises that the efforts they believed were entertaining, even important, would find an audience. Ren thought they had a better chance of winning the lottery than of seeing their names make it into movie theaters.

She had a rule that you couldn't talk about a project

until you had the check in hand. And even that wasn't a guarantee. But at least a check gave some sense of legitimacy. Ren felt she needed a large drink when she overheard Lou telling someone that she'd gotten a part in a new production of *The Marriage of Bette and Boo,* which in truth she'd only auditioned for. With his own career on hold, he now seemed to be banking on hers. She wondered if he'd mention his teaching stints at the New School, these days his only income. Suddenly she felt such tenderness for him she forgot her own awkwardness and had to fight an impulse to hug him, make him spill his drink as he talked to his cohorts.

The guests were directed toward chairs angled at a view of the Hudson. The sun was starting to wash the sky with a peach-pink when the groom, the celebrity producer, appeared. Ren thought he looked good — tanned, but not dangerously so, fit, his graying hair striking against his black tuxedo.

The first touches of red stretched into the evening as Suzette made her way through the formation of chairs. Ren elbowed Lou. He hadn't told her. Suzette looked about twenty years old. With her fine-featured face, her blonde hair silky as a child's, and outfitted in layer upon layer of white, Suzette was so stunning that the guests, Ren included, caught their breaths. Ren changed her impression of Richard to elderly as he turned to Suzette. At that angle his chin looked soft, melting into his neck.

During the ceremony, as the colors of the sunset lengthened and deepened, a baby fussed, then cried outright. By the time Richard and Suzette kissed, the sky had dissolved to a spectacular crimson. The ceremony was completely Hollywood, perfectly orchestrated from costumes to setting.

As Ren and Lou went through the receiving line, Ren wondered if Suzette had been a "hungry girl". At each opening of Lou's plays she'd seen young women anxious and ready to attract the playwright, to do anything to further their careers. The "hungry girls" usually wore tight sweaters and had bright eyes, fly-away hair. They moved their hands and their breasts when they talked. They were prepared to overlook the band of gold on Lou's finger. He dismissed them, he told Ren, because under normal circumstances, without the aura of success around him, the gorgeous women wouldn't even give him a glance.

One of the hungry girls was not easily discouraged. She was just out of college and not unattractive. She attended every performance of Lou's play, *Fortunes*, stood at the back of the theater and grabbed him at intermission. During a mid-week performance Ren had felt the girl's gaze herself. She had looked back at the woman leaning suggestively against a far wall near the fire exit until the girl finally shook a lock of fair hair across her face. That was the last Ren had seen of her, though Lou said she'd popped up in the dressing room during the final performance.

She took Suzette's delicate hand in congratulations. In comparison, Richard's hand was huge, the shake determined. After they'd moved off from the bride and groom, Lou squeezed Ren's wrist briefly, a sign that he was leaving her for a few minutes. While he was gone, Ren imagined the flower-strewn path the beautiful young bride would trod as the spouse of a successful producer. Once Ren had gotten a part in *A Doll's House* solely because she was Lou's wife. The director who'd hired her made no pretense about hoping to work with Lou at some future point. Probably the director had considered her another of the hungry girls. Ren couldn't deny that she was hungry but she wasn't a "hungry girl". There was a difference.

As the guests sipped champagne, a woman in a gold backless evening gown began to sing, rhyming "join" with "coin". Ren vaguely recognized the self-assured yet only passable voice. After a few minutes she asked Lou, "Isn't that Richard's ex-wife?"

"Good recall," Lou said, and Ren could see that he'd been trying to recognize her himself.

"I don't get it," Ren whispered. She paused from further comment as she watched the groom kiss his ex-wife on the shoulder at the song's conclusion. "It's too . . . too civilized."

"Money tends to do that," Lou said. "Makes people lose their passion, if they ever had any." It was the first time Lou had spoken disparagingly of the producer.

On the way into the dining room, Ren listened to an irritated woman. "When I was at Tony and Leslie's wedding in Switzerland there was never a line for anything. I don't know how they managed that but it was wonderful." The woman's tiny red fingernails, almost like droplets of blood with the cuticles bitten and torn, clashed with her carefully made-up face.

The last wedding Ren had been to was Lou's cousin's. Lou's sixty-year-old Aunt Babe, who'd been put to bed drunk, shimmied out of her room and appeared naked in the lobby of the hotel where the out-of-town guests had been staying.

Lou pressed up beside Ren. "The new wife's going to have her own writing room," he whispered.

"Suzette?" Ren asked. "I took her for an actor."

"Actor-cum-writer," Lou said as he described the two-tiered office setup, complete with a "computer loft". "I don't know, Ren. I think we may have been going about this business the hard way."

But that was ridiculous. Marriages like this one couldn't be counted on to weather turmoil; they were temporary arrangements until the parties got the status or the roles or the approval that they wanted. The groom had been married three times already. The average length of a Hollywood marriage was probably no more than eight months.

Dinner wasn't a choice of chicken or beef, accompanied by green beans with slivered almonds. This feast had food stations — seafood, pasta, Japanese and Mexican specialties at each of the corners of the immense ballroom. Three couples already seated at the large round table introduced themselves, then went on with their discussions about childcare arrangements.

Ren tried to avoid the baby talk and concentrate on the variety of foods on her plate, savoring one taste after another. But as she narrowed her favorites down, she found herself distracted by views on toilet training and hand-mouth coordination. When the conversation turned to breast-feeding, Ren set her fork down and listened.

One of the mothers said her baby had just started to talk. The others interjected, proudly revealing their babies' first words: goat, car phone, boo-boo. Ren methodically finished off each portion but no longer tasted the differences among garlic mashed potato, farfalle, or halibut with black bean sauce.

Lou got up to revisit the pasta station and on his way was snagged by the groom. Lou gestured for Ren to join them. Walking in their direction, Ren entertained the idea that the groom might ask about her career, if anything she'd done could translate into a movie. Maybe he wanted to question her availability for a modest role in a new project. Maybe that project would be an artistic, independent film.

"Richard doesn't believe me," Lou said, putting his arm around Ren. "Tell him how long our honeymoon was."

"About nine months," Ren said, disappointed.

Richard said, "I've heard the length of the honeymoon is directly proportional to the success of the marriage."

"Longer means better?" Ren asked.

"Longer means better," Richard said. "How long have you two been married?"

Usually the question made Ren feel old but today she wanted to be funny. She wanted to say, since Suzette was in diapers, but she cleared her throat and answered simply, "In October it'll be seventeen years." Even as she spoke, she realized in a flash that she was talking about an accomplishment, not merely a test of endurance.

"My God," Richard said, "I had no idea." He looked from her to Lou and back again as he explained that even his first marriage had lasted only seven years. Finally, he congratulated them.

"I think he meant it," Ren said as she and Lou meandered back to their table.

"What?" Lou asked, touching her shoulder.

"The congratulations."

They sat down among the couples again. In a stage whisper, the woman with severely cut, short red hair, said to Ren, "You'll see how it is when you have a baby."

Ren thought that if the woman knew how long she and Lou had been married she might assume that one of them was infertile or there had been complications. Ren hadn't told the woman she didn't have any children, that she might never have any, that the theater came first. Childlessness, Ren thought, was probably written across her face. She took a healthy swig of her wine as the red-haired woman, explaining that she was still breast-feeding, drank water from her cut-glass goblet.

Ren tried to see her table as it might appear on stage. Women nearing or just past forty who'd spent their youths as struggling actors or writers or directors. Now they burped babies, changed diapers, saved for college. They made child-rearing seem the more noble work. The zeal with which the women spoke put Ren in mind of being "born again". And yet, though they complained of exhaustion, the women appeared at ease with their choices. Only the main character, Ren herself, past her prime, was still holding out for a breakthrough part that would brighten her future with stage lights.

From the bridal table, speeches began. Jokes. Humorous comments. Someone referred to the groom as a cat with a potential for nine "wives".

"I can't believe it," Lou said. "Everybody's doing stand-up."

The groom raised his hand, toasted his friends, the comedians, his guests, then his new wife. He cleared his throat. "I'd also like to toast a marriage that's endured. Unlike so many things these days," he said. Somebody chuckled but Richard forged ahead. Behind him, Suzette, her face and gown pictures of perfection, gave Richard her complete attention.

"To Lou and Renata who've been married nearly seventeen years," Richard said. "Stand up, you two," he called.

As Renata pushed back from her place at the table, people cheered and hooted, even the red-haired tablemate who was searching for a breast pump under the table. Smiling into the nameless faces around her, Ren was struck by the possibility that a glittering profession might not be her greatest accomplishment.

For the rest of the evening, strangers approached Ren and Lou with congratulations. A man asked Ren to dance and said simply, "The Marriage Lady," leading her onto the floor. Other men cut in as if she had some secret they could extract or maybe they wanted to break the magic down, examine its component parts. An actor she recognized from *L.A. Law* monopolized her for three straight dances. "Give me a few pointers," he begged repeatedly.

Lou stood back and watched her, his arms folded across his chest. He was grinning. The newlyweds were nowhere in sight.

17
The Agent

The second week teaching a writing class at the West Side Y, Lou noticed the woman, the kind a man could coerce. The student was extremely thin, the sharpness of her elbows and facial bones, and probably her knees, likely to stab anyone who pressed too close. Her dark hair was shoulder-length, strawlike, as if what little protein she allowed her body never made it down the length of the filaments. She held her eyes open wide in constant surprise.

The woman seemed aware of her vulnerability, and from the way she looked directly at him, not dropping her gaze shyly, he sensed that she was capable of hanging on. When Lou explained that to be successful as a writer, you needed not only talent but persistence, she nodded. During class she didn't speak up, either to challenge his broad statements or to answer his more specific queries, but sucked in his words. He could almost see the trail of concentration, a thick ribbon of energy winding from her face to his.

Afterward as Lou gathered his papers and a published version of *Daily Life,* she came up and asked if she could meet him before class the following week. She offered to buy him dinner if he would fill her in on the initial class she'd missed. Her assured voice and forthrightness surprised him. But in the seconds before he replied, he noted that she scratched nervously at her thumb with her index finger. A mole the size of a button on a TV remote sat so prominently to one side of her nose, he wondered how she avoided looking at it cross-eyed.

"That won't be necessary," Lou said, reaching for his overcoat.

"It's no problem," she said. Her eyes were gray. "It's the least I can do. And with that long trip you have to make into town."

He didn't remember mentioning his hour-and-a-half commute to the YMCA in Manhattan. Lou slipped into his coat and felt around in his pockets for his gloves, as if winter garb would buffer him not only from the elements but from the odd woman standing before him.

"You don't remember me, do you?" she asked after he finally agreed to meet her in the coffee shop across the street before the next class.

He slowly shook his head and narrowed his eyes, thinking back to the months just before his one film had been released. He'd been thirty-nine, and had met more people working on *Cornered* than he had all the rest of his life. Everyone had wanted a piece of him then — editors, writers, insurance people, brokers. Agents.

"What's your name?" he asked. He was becoming increasingly warm in the down-filled coat.

"Ione," she said and handed him her registration card. It was barely legible.

FOR THE NEXT FEW days, Lou puzzled over Ione. Once his wife said, "You must be at work on a new play. You're so, so . . . preoccupied." Lou patted Renata's hand. What he most appreciated about his wife was also what annoyed him — her unflagging optimism. He hadn't written or thought about writing an original play in over a year.

On Friday afternoon they left for Cape Cod where

Lou would spend the weekend reviewing two resorts for a travel magazine, a promotion First Federal offered its VISA gold card members. The job was compensation from a television producer for whom Lou had written two treatments on spec, neither of which had passed network approval. Every weekend all winter Lou stayed in exquisite accommodations and ate delicious food, and at the end of the winter would receive a four-thousand-dollar check for less than four thousand words.

Because Lou was required to rate and rank the resorts, they all competed for his approval, which ultimately translated into the disposable income of the gold card carriers. Although he imagined his reviews were inconsequential, he enjoyed the routine chilled bottles of wine, platters of cold cuts or fruits and boxes of candies that arrived at his suites. The courting reminded Lou of the festive days after his agent, Miles Scott, had cut a film deal for *Blue Corners*.

Three inches of snow lay on the ground and it was still falling as Renata and Lou packed their rental car. Driving the back roads, Lou studied the sky for patches of blue but it remained dull with the threat of a substantial storm. When they crossed into Massachusetts, I-91 suddenly became more difficult to negotiate. The lines separating the lanes blurred, then disappeared and traffic slowed. The world beyond the car was so still it made him think of a front-row seat at a silent movie.

"I guess I should have sprung for the four-wheel drive," Lou said. "This one's got tires the size of dinner plates. There's no way it can handle any accumulation."

"There's not supposed to be any accumulation," Renata said.

"It's snowing like a bitch," Lou said, and turning to her switched on the windshield wipers, which smeared the icy precipitation across his line of vision. "Why do I put myself through this?" he asked, and, for some weird reason, the odd student's face, her thin wrists, that disfiguring mole, came back to him.

After an equally grueling ride home on Sunday, they found that snow had built up on their roof and moisture darkened the far corner of their bedroom ceiling. "Shit," Lou said softly. "One more problem."

"More?" Renata asked. "What else is wrong?"

LOU WASN'T SURE he'd remember her face; he'd forgotten her name a couple of times over the course of the week. But he spotted Ione immediately sitting against the window of the restaurant. Bent over a cup of tea that smelled of cooking flowers, she smoked a Merit Light.

"Well?" she said, then removed her red felt hat, which set her unruly hair free. Her clavicle protruded so dramatically just above the neckline of her red sweater that Lou wanted to offer her the menu.

"Well," he said.

"You really don't remember me, do you?" She had a pencil in her hand and touched the eraser to the mole on her nose.

"I'm afraid . . ." he said.

"Don't be afraid. Let me make this easy. Miles Scott."

Miles, Lou's ex-agent, was a heavy man a few years younger than Lou. Leading with his midsection, he wore his girth with an aura of importance. During the many meals Lou had with Miles, the man hadn't eaten or drunk excessively. Lou deduced that Miles's weight was just another accoutrement of his power. He lived for the big deals.

Ione said, "Your house five years ago." She sipped her tea. "The salmon stuck to the grill. The corn went up like torches."

Before he could question her, she said, "I had blonde hair then."

Miles had always been with a different woman, usually very young and svelte, when he and Lou got together. The one visit to Lou's house, Miles had been accompanied by a woman much plainer than the rest of the harem. Initially Lou had been moved by the long-term friendship; the woman began telling stories of their college days together, how they'd both been part of the debate team in high school, which eventually won the Pennsylvania state championship. She frequently touched Miles affectionately as she spoke. Lou imagined the couple as students, their odd looks cementing their relationship.

"I thought your name was Karen."

"Carol," Ione said. "I changed it after Miles dumped me." She poked her French fries with a fork.

"How long has that been?" She was much thinner now, her skin almost translucent, her hair out of control but her every move purposeful. And he would have remembered the mole.

"About as long as you've been without an agent."

In those days with Miles, Lou had believed his film was just the beginning; Miles had promised him that success was imminent. And then after mixed reviews, studio interest slowed down to rewrites of other people's screenplays, unanswered phone calls. Finally, Miles stopped calling, too. Often the agent didn't return Lou's calls for weeks. Lou left the agency three times, but was repeatedly wooed back by the potential for writing assignments. And then two and one-half years ago, Lou had written Miles a letter officially terminating the relationship. Miles called Lou to say he was sorry but there it was. By then Miles was a big player, taking a four-months' vacation in the Hamptons. His clients were all celebrities, "money magnets" Miles called them.

Remembering those last dealings with Miles, Lou felt sympathetic to Ione. After that dinner at their house, she'd excused herself and gone into the bathroom. As Miles talked about his upcoming trip to St. Bart's, Lou looked beyond him at the open bathroom window. Cigarette smoke poured out, which Lou took to mean that Miles forbade Ione to smoke in his presence.

"Since when are you interested in writing?" Lou asked Ione. She'd moved her meal around on the plate but hadn't eaten any of it.

"Since now," she said, looking at Lou straight on. "I want to be such a good writer that Miles will beg to represent me."

"Well, let's get started," Lou said and rose to leave.

Lou was paying when Ione said, "I can see his office from my apartment. I know that pile of manuscripts on his desk. I recognize the women who go in and out."

Lou avoided pursuing the subject. "Hey," he said, holding the door for Ione, "I was supposed to fill you in on the first class, remember?"

"I remember everything," she said.

DURING THE FIFTH CLASS of the workshop, Ione's piece was critiqued. Her monologue on a driving trip in Nova Scotia climaxed during an encounter with two drunken Canadians. Lou remembered the story even though Miles had relayed it somewhat differently. Miles told stories for their entertainment value; his version contained none of the terror coloring Ione's.

The criticism of the piece was hard. Someone actually said that it sounded like propaganda for the NRA; Ione had ended the scene with a character deciding to reverse her stand on handguns. Ione didn't respond to the negative comments but looked out the window and absently pulled at her hair or scratched at her thumb.

When the class was over, Ione remained in her seat at the back of the room. Lou felt the intense focus of her gaze. When he looked at her, she was holding her fingers in a gun formation.

She said, "I just wish parents would teach their kids the facts of life."

He studied her. She went on, "I'm not talking about what body part goes where. But that people can get hurt. We're violent creatures. It has nothing to do with TV."

"You should have spoken up."

"I was preoccupied with the slam dunk they gave my work." Ione lit a cigarette although the YMCA had strict no-smoking rules. Her lime green sweater drooped off her shoulder. Without her clothes, she'd be a framework of bones. Lou couldn't see her making love with Miles. The man could crush her.

Ione stared at Lou for an abnormally long time. "There's these pansy asses that can't stand to see their cat kill a mouse. They can't understand it," she said. Despite her size, Ione spoke fiercely. "Wake up call," she said loudly. "It's dangerous out there. We're all in danger if we take our headphones off long enough to listen."

Lou knew she was annoyed partly because of the criticism of her work. He was not unfamiliar with students' tears after a tough evaluation but Ione was unnaturally agitated. Lou thought ahead to what might calm her down, get her out of the classroom and into the street. Or even how he could tactfully change the subject. But suddenly she slipped out of her seat and called as she went out the door, "See you next week."

LOU AND REN SPENT the following weekend trying to stay on Vermont's snow-encrusted roads as they worked their way toward The Madison Inn. By Sunday evening Lou was on the roof of his house chipping the ice buildup from the gutters. Ren handed him dry gloves through the window and urged him to come inside. His arms and hands shook.

"If I don't take care of this, we're going to keep getting leaks in our bedroom," he said. His eyebrows and mustache felt frozen.

On Tuesday he took an early train into New York so that he could prepare for class. Two blocks from the Y, on the southern edge of Central Park, Lou found Ione walking alongside.

"Ione, I'll meet you in class."

"I won't be in class."

"No? Is something wrong?" He stared at the mole on her nose, which appeared more prominent each week.

"I'm dropping the class," she said simply. "But I want to tell you a couple of stories about Miles first," she said. Lou, startled, stopped.

"I don't know that I want to think about him anymore, Ione. He's in my past."

"He's a bisexual," she said.

"What?" Was Ione crazy?

"He disposed of me because I knew too much."

"I'd think he'd want to hold onto you if he thought you'd embarrass him," Lou said, trying to tamp her paranoia.

"He paid me to be quiet," she said.

"Well, you're better off without him," Lou said, now walking quickly toward his class.

Keeping up with Lou, Ione said she was dropping the class because she knew now that her limited talent wouldn't win Miles. "It's going to take a lot more time than I have to get him back," she said.

"Maybe you need to get on with your life," Lou said.

She ignored his comment. "There's these little clusters of women all over the country. They used to be called coffee klatches and now they call them study groups or reading groups."

A sharp wind stung Lou's face as Ione talked.

"They're nothing more than an excuse for women to get together and whine about men. Like they say men think of politics as a competitive sporting event. Or they say, 'That's a book only men will like.' Or, 'You have to be a woman to appreciate this'."

"It's all bullshit," she yelled. Her gray eyes darted around. Lou nervously glanced at his watch.

"Do you know who makes the biggest gulf between the sexes?" she asked, stomping her foot. Lou knew she'd tell him whether he wanted to know or not.

"Women who have a few kids and whose marriages have run out of steam," she said. "They're women who had children in the first place because they never found their true love," Ione said. He noticed an intermittent tic in her right eye.

"Or settled for the wrong one?" Lou asked, trying to wind up the conversation, but Ione didn't seem to hear him.

"I found my true love," she said, her voice slow and deep. "Unfortunately, he doesn't think so."

"Miles is an asshole," Lou said, thankful to pin Ione's state to something he knew to be true.

"But it's not because he's a man," Ione said. She lit another cigarette off the butt she'd nearly finished. "If it was just because he's a man, I wouldn't even think about killing him."

Two days later Ione called Lou at home. "Lou, I think I might take the class again."

"What?" He'd been secretly glad to be rid of her. "Listen," he said, "you can't keep going back and forth on this. There are procedures when you drop or pick up a class."

"I don't care about procedures. I care about Miles," she said. Lou could hear her strike a match. "And you should, too."

— 165 —

"I'm not mad at Miles."

"Are you out of your mind? If he'd gotten behind *you*, you'd have a career now instead of . . . Oh, just forget it," she said and hung up.

Lou told Ren about Ione. He said, "Remember the time Miles came to dinner? The meal caught on fire and the woman Miles brought with him snuck off to smoke." Ren remembered at once.

"She's enraged with Miles," Lou said. "And she thinks I should be, too."

LOU WALKED A DIFFERENT route to his next class. With an inch of fresh snow stuck to every surface, he imagined Ione trailing his footprints. Thoughts of the bizarre woman distracted him during class. He wasn't surprised when she appeared as he was leaving the building.

"Your life's too careful," she challenged him. "To be a writer you have to live on the edge. You have to be angry." Lou walked away from her, but she followed. "I bet you back into parking spaces, have 1.2 drinks at night. I bet you take a stopwatch to your gutter to see if it drains properly."

"Ione," he said stopping, "Don't bitch at me because you're angry with Miles."

She plucked at her eyelashes with the hand not holding the cigarette. "I'm angry because you accepted his rejection."

Lou spoke, trying to appear calm. "My situation with Miles is a completely different scenario." He paused. "For one, I didn't sleep with him." Lou waited for her to laugh but instead she searched her pockets for another cigarette.

"A lot of men have," she said simply. "That's his problem."

"Ione, maybe you should talk to someone." To her, Miles was a monster devouring the world. Lou thought of the pretty boys and slender girls she associated with the agent, and their disappearance when he tired of them.

"I'm talking to *you*," she said.

"I'm hardly a professional," he said, backing off. "Besides, I'm not getting paid."

"I want to handle this myself," she said. "I want to have control over my emotions, not pass them on to some schlub who dilutes them into little farts of feeling."

"Well, let me offer one bit of advice. Move out of the apartment facing his office."

"I'M WORRIED she's going to do something crazy," Lou said to Ren while navigating a four-wheel drive rental over dangerous Maine back roads toward northern New Hampshire. He hadn't heard from Ione in three weeks.

"Just don't get involved," Ren said. "Keep out of it as best you can."

It was like telling him not to get involved in the snow. Everything in front of and behind them was white and gray, like Ione's smoking. Even the sky was hazy with flurries. A van was stuck up ahead of him, and Lou applied the brakes lightly. The Bronco immediately began thumping. As Lou tried to remain calm and pump the brakes, the back of the vehicle swung into oncoming traffic. He swerved out of the path of a station wagon and pulled into a gas station.

Ren said, "We must have lost the road a few miles back. Maybe when the road forked by that barn."

"What barn?" Lou said.

The quality of a resort seemed to correspond proportionally higher to their difficulty in reaching it. The Cedars, which had involved the most treacherous drive to date, had its own power plant, its own telephone system, a regal dining room, sitting rooms filled with polished nostalgia.

After dinner, Lou opened the window of their room slightly and brushed away a hill of snow. After he'd secured the window, he produced two cigarettes.

"Where did you get them?" Ren asked.

"Ren, they're cigarettes. Not dope."

Radio reports of twenty-two inches of new snow woke them.

"I've got to get back for my class," Lou said. "We can't get snowed in."

While Ren was unpacking late that night after another harrowing drive, Lou stepped on a cold wet spot on the bedroom floor. The damp shadows on the walls and ceiling had spread. Door jambs wept. He climbed onto the roof and began hacking away again at the layers of ice and hardened snow.

His gloves were soaked and his glasses fogged up from his breath. If Miles hadn't bungled the contract on the second movie option, he would have a new roof, one that didn't leak. And if Miles had really done his job, he and Renata would be spending winters in the Caribbean, warming themselves far from dripping roofs and slippery New England roads.

His hands were numb with cold, his mustache and nose hairs stiff. As he drove a few blows, he imagined he was pounding Miles's desk. Lou thought of Miles's jowls, his protuberant stomach and thick neck, and struck the ice a final blow, seeing Miles's blood stain the white of the roof.

As THE WINTER was coming to a close, Lou began to look forward to climbing outside and onto the roof to be alone with his dangerous daydreams. Sometimes he stopped chopping to have a smoke in the cold solitude. By the end of the month, he put in a claim with the insurance company to have the bedroom repainted and spackled and some of the molding replaced. And still he hadn't heard from Ione.

At the beginning of April, when New York was enjoying a false spring, Lou gave a brief final class and two of his best students brought copies of *Daily Life* for him to sign. Lou was elated as he walked along Broadway, the street lively with people, forsythia brightening the cityscape, the air comfortably warm on his face.

"Hey," a voice called. Surprised that he felt relief, relief that Ione's anger hadn't been transformed into tragedy, he greeted her enthusiastically.

Her hair looked somehow softer as it blew against her smile; she appeared uncharacteristically calm and was dressed entirely in black. Her tiny pink abstract pin caught his attention.

"Your last class?" she asked, and he was taken aback. Nothing was spontaneous about her; Ione could turn coincidence into a complex plot.

"So, how have you been?" he asked, reluctant to ask a more specific question.

"Terrific," she said. "Miles and I are back together."

Lou was overcome with sympathy. He pitied the woman, condemned to living continually with that giant blob of dismissiveness. He put his arms around her, certain she received no such tenderness from the agent. Miles would discard Ione again, the only question was when.

"I'm not serious," Ione said, wiggling out of his embrace. "The truth is, I just moved out of the apartment across from Miles's office."

Instinctively, he bent forward to hug her again, but this time more like someone who'd witnessed a child conquering a two-wheeler. "Ione, that's wonderful."

She opened her hand. Flat in her palm lay two keys. "I have copies. Come on." When he hesitated, she said, "Fifteen minutes. And I swear I'll never bother you again for the rest of your life."

"You don't need to be so dramatic," he said but she'd already started walking. He'd look at the apartment and still be able to make his usual train home.

As she sliced through the crowds and crossed streets against red lights, he followed her small form. He did want to see evidence that she was getting her life together. Selfishly, he hoped she wouldn't take the opportunity to show him something else that she'd written. Or to make a pass. But that would have come up before now. Besides, what could happen in fifteen minutes? Lou pursued Ione as if he would be punished if he let her out of his sight.

At an old building with broken tiles in the entranceway, she paused for him to catch up, then inserted her key. Their feet echoed in the stairwell. "Wait'll you see this view," she said.

"What's wrong with the elevator?" he called. She was ahead of him still.

"Elevators make me nervous," she said.

He heard her key metaling its way into a lock of a door on the fourth floor.

"Tah dah," she said, swinging the door open. The rooms were completely empty, the old wooden floors scarred. Lou spotted a balled-up Kleenex in the corner.

"So, this is the new place," he said.

"No, it's the old place," she said coolly and he felt a chill go through his body. He was back on the desolate snow-covered roads, trapped in the leaking ordeal of the winter months.

She handed him a pair of binoculars.

Before he took them, Lou said on an exhale, "Miles."

The plot had circled back to its beginning. So absorbed in the progression of events, he'd forgotten about structure. Lou looked through the binoculars and studied the office he knew well. He saw the straight-back chair he'd sat in countless times as Miles made calls and deals and screamed at other clients. Lou looked at the two-drawer file cabinet up against Miles's desk, still overrun with man-uscripts.

Miles had his suit jacket off when he came into Lou's view. His stance, his suspenders, his prominent middle, were unmistakable. A second man stood in the doorway. A rush of sadness blew over Lou. He became aware of Ione breathing heavily behind him. With two hands she was holding a revolver. A .38.

"Ione," he said softly. The gun was huge in her small hands. "Where in the hell did you get that?"

"I bought it," she said. "It's legal." After a pause, she said, "I've thought this whole thing out." She turned and with difficulty opened the window. Lou sat frozen in place, looking across the busy street, letting the scenario work itself out as Ione had planned.

Ione knelt by the window, extended her unsteady arms. Slowly Lou approached her. She looked so innocent fumbling at the window that he found himself showing her how to support her arms against the sill. Take aim.

She held the gun in place and whispered, "Call him."
"What?"

"Call him. I can't get him in focus if he's moving all over the office."

Lou smelled sweat and realized that it was his own. Glimpsing at Ione's profile, he noticed the mole and won-dered if it would interfere with her aim.

"He's at the desk now," Lou said.

"Just call him," she repeated.

An old rotary phone sat on the floor. Lou pulled it to him and slipped his finger into the sequence of numbers he easily remembered. The number on which he'd once pinned his future. Watching the office across from him as he dialed, he felt himself directing the determining scene of his life.

He had felt that same excitement when he was writing.

The phone rang in Lou's ear; Miles reached to answer it; Lou hung up; a gun roared. Quickly, Ione fired twice more, the shots burrowing into the cement above and on either side of Miles's office. Lou lunged at her and pressed her to the floor. Listening to their hearts pounding then to the traffic below, Lou fantasized taking up the .38 and firing accurately. But instead, he gathered Ione in his arms as if she were a daughter caught in a nightmare.

He stroked the hair away from Ione's damp face, murmured "Shh, shh," and let his hand rest on her forehead. Across the street, the scene was unflappable. Miles picked up the phone again.

Gently, Lou uncurled Ione's fingers from the gun and pushed it across the room. Looking down at her, now nestled quietly in his arms, he felt a flash of happiness. Her tiny wrists were warm. He held her until his hands stopped shaking.

18

Closing

I know now that a lot of our trouble came from ordinary bad luck. An accumulation year after year pressed us closer to the edge of the precipice. The good happened in the same way, visiting us in a rush of fortuitous circumstances that at once amazed and terrified us. In the end, you could say that our lives were spent tilting between those two extremes that we couldn't control any more easily than icy back roads. We were committed gamblers, our life together the addiction.

Five years after *Cornered* was released, we ran out of money. We'd assumed that digging through coat pockets to buy a pack of cigarettes or a quart of milk was behind us, part of our history. But the needs all returned and humiliation was more acute because, if only for a short while, we'd tasted a life of ease. That life had turned out to be a clear day in early spring, a break between showers.

We were still obligated to a hefty mortgage on our Connecticut house; Lou's new agent was hungry as a dependent; we'd gotten used to eating out, buying gifts and furnishings with the flick of a credit card. Neither of us had worked at a job with benefits in years. We made minimum payments on our debts for as long as we could, our sense that we were buying time soon replaced by the feeling that we were doing time.

We tried praying to St. Jude, which Lou had resorted to years earlier, right before the deal for *Cornered* was orchestrated. St. Jude, help of the hopeless. We said the prayer separately and together nine times a day for a week. I trained myself to recite it in one sustained exhalation; it soon became part of my breathing. After I told Lou that our petition might not be considered coming from the hopeless, I began to make pacts with God. The promises all involved sacrificing my acting.

Nothing worked. Our losses grew from a pileup into a wall we couldn't move — the Writer's Guild went on strike; the new agent died of AIDS; the two leads and coproducers of Lou's made-for-TV movie started divorce proceedings; I developed "throat tension" and lost my voice-overs; I gained fifteen pounds. Like the rest of the country, Hollywood cut back drastically on funding for new projects, particularly anything considered off center.

We attempted to hold onto the house, that visible symbol of our personal life. I rescheduled auditions around my paying jobs — a temporary long-term assignment typing for an insurance firm, and reading play scripts at fifty bucks a shot.

Each morning I woke at four to read through scripts, and by seven-thirty was in the car playing hard rock to clear my head of character motivations and stage directions. The jolting lyrics emptied my mind of dialogue, leaving it clear for thoughts of maximum benefit period, prior earnings, deferred compensation, credit disability.

As I became caught in a frantic schedule that left no room for rehearsals even if I were offered a role, Lou found himself with more and more free time. The class he'd been teaching in the city was canceled. I'd imagine Lou upstairs in his study willing the phone to ring, to prove that he was still part of someone else's plans.

Lou stopped reading and watching reviews of any

kind. He started his boycott the evening an *Entertainment Tonight* reporter flicked her streaked hair while assessing a new release a friend of his had written. She said simply, "Travesty," as if it were the punch line to a joke.

When Lou talked to fellow writers, his normally sharp memory failed; he frequently forgot the names of particular movies or actors. I'd lived with Lou for almost twenty years. I'd learned to predict his reaction to comments and criticism better than my own. When his ironic edge, so crucial to the humor in his work, began to erode, I didn't know how to cope. How could I react to him when he had willingly stopped reacting?

He took a job at The Nutmeg Liquor Store stocking shelves, signing for deliveries, loading liquor purchases into Mercedes and Porsches, and occasionally working the cash register. He accepted the job after a discussion with himself: "What else can I do? (Pause) I can write and I can do manual labor." Teaching and editing had proved to be unreliable sources of income.

Off-Broadway gossip was replaced by tales of insurance rip-offs and liquor sales. Lou mentioned the Nutmeg's regular customers not by name but by their purchases. The short dark-haired, fifty-year-old mechanic who frequented the store every evening after work was known as "Six of Bud, pack of Winstons, two Quik Piks." The physical world seemed to have a cleansing effect on Lou. The closer he got to raw physicality, the briefer his tolerance for false hopes.

The store was so small that Lou spent most of his time moving boxes, repositioning displays and restocking the shelves. Each workday, all spring and summer as the apple tree filling our kitchen window thickened with fruit, my forty-five-year-old playwright came home from work with a different part of his body throbbing. Shoulder, elbow, wrist, ankle, fingers. In reaction, I made love too carefully. If I forgot about the purple abrasion on Lou's upper thigh, I might hear him catch his breath in sudden pain and I'd be snatched from my own pleasure.

In the few free hours when we once discussed movies and plays and books, Lou took on odd jobs for the liquor store customers. He'd paint their manorial living and dining rooms, lower their ceilings, varnish their woodwork. Those nights he returned home more stooped than ever, his whole body in trauma.

Oddly, to get through the long hours of hefting cases of wine and beer and liquor, Lou thought only of statistics, not of how he could turn this experience into a screenplay. He would ask me, "At what age do you think the average male buys the most alcohol?" "Do you think all the beers we've drunk since we've been married would fill these two rooms?" "Do you know the percentage of homeowners who have to call a professional after they've tried to do a home repair themselves?"

One day, the phone did ring. Would Lou be interested in writing a screenplay about a group of homeless people who start a baseball team? While Lou was in New York meeting with the development people, in my swivel chair at the insurance company I petitioned God again. At the very moment that I was begging for our lives, a twenty-five-year-old producer was telling Lou she wondered if he could be funny enough for the project. When Lou got off the train from New York, he drove to the liquor store and single-handedly stocked seventy-five cases of liter-and-a-half wine bottles in two hours. Then he drank a liter by himself. He could hardly move when he returned home that night. He asked me to untie his shoes. And we knew finally that we were torturing ourselves beyond endurance.

The afternoon we discussed moving far enough away for two low-level jobs to allow us extra each week for a pizza, we sat on our front porch. We looked at each other and then we looked out on all that was ours. Legions of trees stood tall and impenetrable on three sides of the property. An old stone wall visible through the leafy border matched the smaller stones circling our flower gardens. The cedar-sided house blended into bark at the end of a dirt road. We had discovered this spot the way we had discovered each other — by chance, recognizing immediately that we fit.

I'd come to know all the trees — the birches and beeches and maples, the twin tulipwood, the evergreens nibbled in winter by brazen deer. The apple tree's over-ripe fruit struck the ground like an erratic clock. The 20-foot black oak at the entrance to our house — the centerpiece of our property — scratched at the upstairs windows as if wanting to be let in. With first light each morning that tree greeted me like a pet, a pet that asked nothing of me.

Within a few days after we decided to sell the house, all the leaves fell off the oak. They were the color of dried blood. Usually the oak leaves were the last to appear and the final ones to loosen their hold. That year they blew off in such steady determination they seemed like early birds heading to warmer climes. In the still darkness of early morning as the leaves flew away, I'd hear the first cry of a veery. If I could have seen it, it would have been a slight curve slicing into the air with silence on either end — a comma, a pause, the imprint of a fingernail against the palm of a clenched fist.

WE TOLD OUR REALTOR, Don David, we were moving to L.A. even though we had no intention of joining west coast unemployment lines. I couldn't keep Don David's name straight. Half the time I called him Don, the other David. He told us that our house required a very special buyer — someone who liked seclusion and nature, unconventional people who didn't require a formal dining room and wall-to-wall carpeting, who preferred the rustic quality of stained barnsiding to lots of light and glass. Someone exactly like us.

After five couples had inspected our house and passed, Don David reported that it was not suitable for a baby.

A baby.

In none of the house plans I'd sketched in the early months of our marriage, in faint pencil on the blank pages of Samuel French scripts, had I ever included room for a child. Pale yellows and pinks and blues never entered my thoughts; all walls I envisioned as ivory, if not wood.

As I had once considered and reconsidered a play part I'd be best for, I began to rethink my decision: Maybe I shouldn't have ruled out that little room. Sometimes, when auditioning, I'd been asked to read a monologue of a character I hadn't prepared for. Even with a cold reading I'd been convincing. Twice, I'd gotten roles that way. And I'd been surprised and exhilarated that I could stretch further than I'd anticipated.

I asked Lou what he thought about extending the family unit. He stared at me for a minute, then looked over my head as if another person were behind me. "Let's give it a shot," he said. Because he responded so quickly, I wondered how long he had been waiting for me to ask that question. Or maybe he was up for trying anything that might fill the hole left from his writing life.

Sometimes a decision isn't as much a choice as a recognition of what's been sitting in front of you all the while. Standing before Lou, handing him the suggestion for our lives to turn down a different road, I saw for the first time the house behind us. From that distance I understood it for what it was. While I had entertained the idea that it had the presence of a person — with its masculine wood interior and feminine gestures in windowsills, curtains, and decorations — I realized now that the house was not the core of our relationship, only the container. The change we'd petitioned for didn't need stage lights or cameras to make it possible.

We had passed the intellectual border into another country. It seemed right that a child — tangible, living — would be the final destination. There we would stop and settle.

THE SATURDAY MORNING my temperature was rising, Don David called to say he'd be bringing "an eager buyer" over in half an hour. An hour later, after eyeing each other and studying our watches, Lou scribbled a note saying the house couldn't be seen until after one o'clock, and stuck it on the door. Then he slid the chain lock.

We went upstairs, got into bed, and immediately fell into each other's needs in a familiar and yet different way. For the first time our lovemaking had a goal other than pleasure. When we heard leaves outside our house rustle and crackle, I imagined a woman in heels walking up the slate pathway to the front door as if she were on ice, the couple peering into the downstairs windows. Lou quickly pulled me back to procreating.

I straddled him, my legs folded on either side, and we stared directly into each other's eyes. He held me by the hips, moved me very slowly at first. Once we had the rhythm, he closed his eyes and sent his hands up along my body. Then, without uncoupling, he turned me on my back and pressed hard, with urgency.

When the realtor returned after one, Lou and I were sitting on the living room couch. I was flushed and smiling. We'd changed our sheets and aired out the bedroom, but the following day we didn't. I liked the idea of strangers looking at our unmade nest still damp with lust. Even when I wasn't ovulating, Lou and I began to rush to bed right before prospective buyers invaded us. Laying claim to our love even though we were about to disappear from that place, we were like animals marking territory with our most intimate scent.

I also began a new acting career. Depending upon the buyers' questions, I was a broken yuppie moving to more unspoiled territory; a transplanted Southerner who wanted to return home; most often Lou and I were on our way to Hollywood.

IN SPRING, I planted the largest vegetable garden I'd ever undertaken. I put peas and onions and lettuce in early and everything else on time, leaving space for bumper crops. The rows of vegetables came through the dark cool earth in long straight lines. And then I thinned the plants out. I knew I hadn't planted the garden to impress prospective buyers. I was looking for real roots to reinforce the metaphorical ones. But I still wasn't pregnant.

We didn't get a chance to taste our tomatoes — Golden Boys and Celebrities, or even the Early Girls. Morons bought our house in June. At the closing, the husband made huge scrawling signatures on the paperwork and the wife had to sign around his sweeping extenders. She was, in fact, one of Lou's customers from The Nutmeg Liquor Store.

After the closing was complete, Lou was morose. He said, "Now *this* is selling out."

OUR LITTLE VINYL-SIDED house in Fallsburg, so far up the Hudson that New York City and Hollywood feel as far away as the moon, is just right. It's a pre-fab that we rent with an option, and all our neighbors know it. There's one five-foot Japanese maple out by the mailbox. Our neighbors sit only about a hundred feet off on either side. Most of the property is behind us — a long thin strip of grassy turf like a miniature golf course that eventually meets up with a pine forest, which, if you close your eyes after a heavy rain, almost smells like Connecticut.

At first we held out hope for that call, the voice that would say, "Lou, Renata, where *are* you two baked potatoes? Come on out. Come on down," or "Come back to us." When that didn't happen, I took a night job at the local newspaper. I said simply that we'd moved from the New York metropolitan area to raise a family. "In God's country," I actually heard myself say.

Lou has his own odd-jobs business, mostly painting. Within a week, nearly all of his shirts and pants were spattered with some degree of paint damage. When I read about a playwriting fellowship he'd be perfect for, he said he wasn't interested. Lou's paychecks are modest, but on time. If he overdoes it on a particularly strenuous job, he'll take a day off to relax. And nobody calls him a misogynist or a bigot or says he's a disgrace to the Catholic Church.

All our extremes are gone — crushing rejection, euphoric recognition. Our up-and-down lives have leveled out into a plain as wide as the Midwest. You can see what's coming from miles away in time to prepare. We feel like recovering alcoholics.

During a sonogram, Lou and I listened to the baby's heart beating. It sounded like a tiny whip lashing out again and again. Like parents, like child, I thought. Striking out, striking on — together.

The baby inside me had all the potential of a brand new character. I'd just gotten the part, but hadn't yet memorized the lines or discovered motivation. But I had the role. To me, that beginning, even more than the final applause, was always the most thrilling part of theater.

Having a child is an ordinary role that feels one-of-a-kind. Lou comes home from putting in a dropped ceiling or paneling or painting a couple of bedrooms, working not so differently from his father. Lou's retiled the bathroom, repapered the baby's room. He's built a deck out back that faces the white pines. He says it almost feels like he added another room onto the house.

And he even made a cradle. When he displayed the finished piece he said, "Ren, I know this is the biggest damn cliché in the world, but didn't it come out good?" As he turned it carefully — the curves and angles perfectly painted — I could visualize the trunk of hardwood where it had started.

Our bed's grown to the size of a field to accommodate us — Lou, me, Grace, Lark and Lucky, the labs. That innocence that cuddles between Lou and me, a meld of our years together, is ours to keep.

Grace.

Every Saturday afternoon when Grace has her nap, Lou and I squeeze into the formica tub with a bottle of wine. Lou tries to pick a different one each week from the local liquor store. We set our glasses on the lip of the tub and talk. Mostly we talk about Grace. Her face, her hands, her sounds for words, when she'll walk. Who she'll become. When we mention a play or an actor now, it's like a nostalgic story that over time and telling has been buffed free of pain. After we dry each other off, we get into bed under fresh sheets in the bright room, turn to each other and close our eyes.

During the week, I spend whole days playing with Grace. I exaggerate my facial expressions. I sing her songs from when I was a little girl. I laugh sometimes, even when there's nothing really funny at all.